Harbor House: Deadly Intentions

Diana Stout

Cover design by R.C. Matthews

Hardcover ISBN-13: 979-8-9936930-2-6
Paperback ISBN-13: 979-8-9870751-6-6
eBook ISBN: 979-8-9936930-3-3

Dedication

To those who enjoy escaping for a few hours and those who enjoy being surprised.

To Freida McFadden, whose early publishing process I discovered had mimicked mine, showing me that it can be done this way. Thank you for your friendship.

And to Sharon McKelvey, Linda Bradley, Lenore English, Mary Fountain, and Jennifer Fountain Snook—special friends and early readers whose comments and enthusiasm were and always are much appreciated.

Contents

Some houses keep secrets. Harbor House keeps them alive.

Harbor House: Deadly Intentions

same family, same house, two stories 100 years apart
split by time

Diana Stout

Part I

Chapter 1

Revenge is a dish best served cold –
Memoirs of Matilda (1846) by Eugène Sue.

Anonymous

Present Day

I've waited a long time to exact my revenge.
Finding the hidden treasure will be a plus.
It won't be long now.

Chapter 2*

1924

Though the first strands of light on the horizon were an hour away, men on Sinclair's docks were boarding boats, preparing for a day on the lake despite the rain and the fog. By the time they were out on the lake, the fog would be gone.

Twice a month, instead of cutting down trees for the mill, they came out of the forest to help supply the cook's store of fish. Even though it was work, it felt like a day off.

A ringing bell cut through the dark. All heads turned toward Harbor House Island—only a quarter mile offshore—even though they couldn't see it. Their boss, Sawyer Van Houten, and his wife, the former Margaret Sinclair, lived on the island, and that bell meant only one thing.

Danger.

Someone was in trouble.

*****

An hour later...

Mike O'Hara, Sawyer's foreman, draped the blanket over Margaret's body as she lay at the foot of her bed. One would think she had just hit her head and died, believing blood had poured out of the wound, pooling beneath her brunette curls.

The slash across her throat said otherwise.

He went downstairs and found a small group of men gathered in the great hallway by the front door, raincoats dripping. Their expressions mimicked his own—frustration and anger. "Has anyone found Sawyer?" Margaret was family to all of them, including her husband.

"No," said a giant of a man named Red because of his Irish red hair. "But, we found an empty rowboat floating out on the lake."

Mike frowned. "But we didn't pass—"

"It was on the east side of the island. It's got a Canadian tug's name on it, but there's no tug anywhere."

"There's no one else in the house or on the grounds," one man said. Other voices were heard, too.

"Except for the baby sleeping upstairs."

"Sawyer's boat is still here."

"Sawyer didn't do this."

"He worshipped them both. He'd do anything to protect them," Mike said.

Red added. "None of this makes sense."

They stood there, looking at each other, all of them feeling helpless.

Mike removed his hat, wiped his forehead, and jammed it back on his head. Hands on his hips, he looked upstairs. "I wonder if we'll ever know what happened here."

Chapter 3

Hunter Marshall

Present Day

"Why are you so upset?" Amanda asks.

I grab her elbow and propel her in front of me into the library's small meeting room that holds a table with half a dozen chairs, a lone trash can in the corner, and a few pictures on the wall, moving us away from the library's front desk where others can hear us.

Letting go of her arm, I shut the door behind me, the skirt of my dress catching in the door. Opening the door a crack, I tug at my dress, re-close the door, and move around the table, shutting the door on the opposite wall, the door that leads into the library's private area where our desks are located.

I turn and face her. "I'm not upset—"

"But, you're not happy either."

"Would you be happy to discover a friend deceived you on your thirtieth birthday?"

Amanda blinks, her lips disappearing as she rolls them inward, biting down on them. Her tell that she's thinking. Then, her mouth twists to one side, then the other. Another tell.

I wait.

Does she think I'm angry with her?

I glance through the door's glass. The front desk is well attended again. We can take a few minutes to talk without harm to any of our patrons.

"You're right. I wasn't looking at it from your point of view. Mars probably wasn't either." Her shoulders slump. A sign she's feeling defeated.

My initial frustration at her question dissipates. Mars Smith and Amanda McFadden are my friends. Best friends. My only friends.

I met them both during the last week of ninth grade, as we enrolled for fall classes, becoming fast friends over summer.

Amanda always reminds me of an Earth or Garden Fairy, who can easily blend into a forest or a field of wildflowers because of her hair and the way she dresses. Ironic because she hates being outside and dislikes most animals.

Mars, on the other hand, loves fashion and aspired to be a Chippendale dancer when we were in school. Back then he was too thin, saying he just wanted their abs. He's got them now. He could be a model with his height and thin but muscular frame. His looks made him popular throughout high school. The girls drooled all over him, but he never noticed them. He preferred being a nerd without a girlfriend. Still does. While he isn't gay, he isn't into girls either. He claims girls want commitments and want to change him, to make him an alpha when he's clearly a beta. Plus, he says he isn't ready to make a commitment of that kind. He likes his freedom and being in control.

We've been a trio ever since. The last thing I ever wanted to do was hurt either of them. Ever.

I go around the table and hug her. Stepping back, I ask, "Can we talk about it later, over dinner?"

She nods. Her mouth opens, then closes. I know exactly what she wants to say, but I pretend I don't.

"Okay to invite Mars?" she finally asks.

I lift one shoulder in a half shrug. Then smile. "Sure." I can't remember when we didn't invite the third person.

She gives me a quick hug, turns, and opens the door, returning to the front desk to help the next patron in line who has a stack of children's books to check out.

Instead of following Amanda to the front desk, I spin around, escaping through the second door. In a few steps, I'm hidden away inside my cubicle where no one can see me.

I need a few minutes and am glad for the gray divider wall that separates me from the rest of the staff. Unlike the other desks that face walls and are in the open, mine has three tall cubicle walls because I'd be exposed to both the outside windows and the small meeting room otherwise. I was told that when another desk became available, I'd be moved, but when the time came, I asked if I could remain here instead. The library director was surprised but let me stay without question.

If anyone were to ask, I always blame being the only child of older parents for my need of privacy, but that excuse is a lie. I just don't want anyone knowing my business even though I have no business worth knowing.

Ironic, yes, I know. But, it fits when others call me an introvert. I can be. I like people well enough and can talk a lot if they ask questions or talk about topics I care about. I'm a neurodivergent if the truth were known. Just on the cusp. Nothing big. Mostly sensory overloads and a fixation on certain topics. Most of which I've kept secret.

I don't know why, but I seem to attract needy people. People who claim they want advice but really don't. People who like to vent but aren't interested in fixing the problem. People who are bored with their lives. Come to think of it, Amanda's like that.

Mom used to say I have an open face. A welcoming face.

To me, it's just a face. Nothing spectacular, but better than average.

The one time Amanda, Mars, and I talked about our looks, Mars told me I had kissable lips. He confided that more than one guy would have liked to get into my pants, but I wasn't into casual meetups. Never have been. Still not, even though I did just turn thirty. I can't say the same for Amanda. She whines that turning thirty means our lives are over. She likes to exaggerate. I sometimes wonder if she shouldn't have found a career on stage.

Mars confided and promised both of us that he'd never reveal our secrets to any of the boys, especially the ones who couldn't figure me out and questioned him all the time. They wanted his help in hooking me up with them. It never happened.

Three weeks after our first connection, we secretly admitted to each other that we weren't like our classmates. None of us felt like we fit in with the others. Mars and Amanda could have easily enough, but for some reason didn't believe they were like their classmates.

I was the outsider, never talking or socializing. I didn't even have a desire to attend any of the proms. Amanda and Mars would go together, but I had no interest.

But overall, we had each other. We were each a slice of the whole. Incomplete without the other two.

I sit at my desk, staring at the framed photograph of the three of us—arms around each other's shoulders with Mars in the middle. I wonder if I could have survived being dumped at the altar almost a decade ago without them, or being ghosted after a year-long relationship a few years ago.

Ever since, I've sworn off men.

Mars wasn't trying to hurt me with his birthday present last night. He loves me. They both do. If not for them, I doubt I could have managed surviving my parents' murders just before my college graduation as well as I did.

Last night, I didn't realize that learning about my heritage was such a trigger.

I left not long after Amanda brought out the cake.

No doubt Mars didn't sleep last night, worrying himself into a panic attack. I need to apologize to him. And, to Amanda.

I'll do it at dinner tonight. Knowing Amanda, she's already called Mars, and we'll be meeting at our favorite deli. The one that has lots of booths with high cubicle-like separation walls.

We each like our privacy. When we're together, we huddle and talk quietly, so no one can hear us. Another reason we're such great friends. We always share everything. At least, I thought we did until last night when Mars dropped a bomb on me.

Chapter 4

Mars Smith

I enter the deli, my gaze going to our preferred booth in the back corner. Empty. I'm the first to arrive. At the booth, I drop my book bag on the table to reserve it, then go to the counter to place my order.

A couple minutes later, Amanda is in line with a few people between us.

Handed the number stand assigned to my meal, I move aside and turn to head back to the booth. Hunter is at the end of the line. She gives me a feeble smile. Her fake smile. I've seen her give it to others often enough to know what it means. Then, it broadens into a genuine smile. One that says she's forgiven me.

Last night, I gave her a birthday present I thought she would love. By the time, she left the party, I could tell she wasn't happy with me. The strange thing is, she never even opened my gift.

At first, she was warm and enthusiastic when I handed her my gift, thanking me.

But, I'll never forget those first few seconds after reading the envelope headline, *DNA Results,* how she blinked a couple times in quick succession, stared at it, and then her fake smile appeared.

I've never liked that smile. Be real is my philosophy. I don't know why she guards her feelings so carefully.

Be real? Sliding into the booth, I nearly laugh out loud. None of us are real. All three of us are guarded. Always have been. Everyone has a secret of one kind or another. All people.

At that point, Amanda shoved her gift into Hunter's hands,

my gift forgotten. And then, Amanda served her homemade birthday cake. Hunter left soon after.

I knew she was annoyed. And I know she knew that I knew she was annoyed. I could see it in her eyes. Afterward, Amanda was aggravated. Hunter had barely touched her cake.

No doubt the reason we're meeting now. To fix last night. Amanda hates any discontent or dissension among us. She's always been the fixer.

The thing I want to know is did Hunter like her gift after opening it when she got home?

What's taking Amanda so long to get here? She should have ordered by now.

Because I sit facing the wall, I twist around so I can see the front counter. No such luck. I'll have to slide out and stand up to look over the wall.

I'm tempted to pull my reading device out of my bag while I wait, but decide against it. I'll no sooner start, and they'll arrive. I go to the restroom to wash my hands instead.

A minute later, I'm back at our booth and still alone. Peering over the booth, I see Amanda with one hip against the counter, talking with Hunter who is paying for her order. Hunter sees me, says something to Amanda who looks over, and then they're talking to each other again.

I slide into the booth. Seconds later, the two of them are sitting opposite me.

"Before either of you say a word," Hunter starts, "I want to apologize."

Her hand is in her purse. I know I'm frowning, but I want to know where this is going before I say anything.

Hunter continues, placing an envelope on the table in front of her.

It's my gift.

She turns the envelope over.

With the company's name and address in the return address corner, the envelope has *DNA Results* printed in big black letters across its width.

Amanda reaches for it and looks at the back. "You didn't even open it?"

"No. I was going to when I got home," Hunter says, "but then realized you both probably wanted to see me opening it. So, I thought I'd wait."

Her gaze is steady and unreadable. I'm glad she's sharing it with us. I want to see her expression when she opens it.

I shrug as if I don't care. "We got too busy getting our sugar high last night."

Amanda laughs. "Yeah, I had to take some aspirin before I went to bed. I ended up with a sugar headache."

"Did you check your blood?" Hunter asks, concerned.

Neither Hunter nor I ever talk about Amanda's weight gain these last few years. She's never been thin and is curvy in all the right places. Most girls would love to have her curves. When her doctor told her at the last exam that she was pre-diabetic, she told us diabetes doesn't run in her family.

Both Hunter and I know she has a secret sugar addiction. No doubt the reason for the weight gain and the new pre-diabetic diagnosis.

Amanda shrugs. "I did and it was okay. I've got to stop eating those gummies."

I know that shrug. She isn't telling the truth. Or, at least, not the whole truth. She should have said gummies, chocolates, and taffy, too.

Amanda claps her hands. "Aren't you going to open the envelope? Mars told me he was getting you something special. "I'm dying to know!"

Hunter appears calm but anxious and curious at the same time. She nods and opens it, pulling out several pages. Silently, she begins reading.

"Read it aloud," I say.

Hunter clears her throat and starts reading every word.

"No, not everything," Amanda cries. "Just the important stuff."

Hunter summarizes. "It's just giving me the usual disclaimer stuff. That the results can change over time depending on how many people provide their DNA in the future. That my nationality percentages will change as I get more connections with people who have submitted their DNA, etc." She looks up at me. "What do they mean by more connections?"

I respond, "It's a website where people create accounts and create family trees. Your DNA shows how you're related to others. Once I signed up and created my family tree, I wondered what yours would look like."

"Why mine and not Amanda's?"

Amanda jumps in. "Your birthday came before mine, Silly Goose. Mars promises to do mine for my birthday."

Hunter passes the page to Amanda who passes it to me. Hunter displays the second page. It's a map and has numbers on various countries.

"It looks like I'm part Dutch, Irish, English, but predominately Scottish.

Again, she passes the page to us.

"This doesn't make sense." She's reading the last page.

"Why not?" I ask.

She hands it to me. I turn it so that I can read.

"It's talking about adoptions and other reasons why I might not have my parent's DNA," she says.

"That's ridiculous," Amanda states.

"Let's look at your account," I say, pulling my laptop out of my book bag.

"I have an account?" Hunter asks.

"It's the only way I could submit your DNA. Besides, I figured you'd want your own family tree."

"So, she has a password and everything?" Amanda asks.

"Yes, once we're in, you can change it to what you want, Hunter."

"But if you sent it in, don't you already know the results," Amanda asks.

"No, while everything was mailed to me, I didn't open it or go online to look."

Hunter's face scrunches up as Amanda and I chat. Her thinking face.

"So, why wasn't I getting any emails from this company if I have an account?"

She isn't just asking a question. She's demanding an answer. It's not adding up. And, she's right.

"I set it up and created a new email account for you. Since you'll want to take charge of the account now, we can change the fake email to your regular one."

"No, that's okay," Hunter says quickly. "I'm okay keeping the account in my name with the email you created for me, but obviously I need to take over the email account, along with this website, and create new passwords."

As I talk, I'm tapping on the keyboard, going to the pages of the website and her email account. I want her to know, to see that before we leave tonight, I will no longer have access to the accounts.

All three of us have excellent technology skills, but I'm the expert. It all started in middle school when I took my first computer class. Later in high school, we ended up in a computer class together and learned about coding, created apps, and even learned some hacking skills outside of class on our own.

Amanda and I continued taking classes together, but Hunter stopped. In that tenth-grade class, we passed notes back and forth on the computers without the teacher ever knowing about the app I had created with the file hidden in the school's system. I, er, we were that good.

Hunter tries pushing Amanda out of the booth. "What are you doing?" she cries.

"I want to see what he's doing. Move over," Hunter demands.

"Wait a minute! I want to see, too! You be in the middle, Mars."

I slide out and Amanda slides in first, then me, then Hunter with my laptop open in front of me. First, we go to her email account. She turns the screen toward her, so we can't see the keyboard as she types in a new password.

Then, they watch as I sign into the website, where again she hides the keyboard while she changes the password.

I show Hunter how to go to the family tree I started for her.

She points at the screen, at lines that radiate from her picture.

"You've got Mom and Dad as my parents and it's one connective line, but what's this other connective line with just a question mark?"

"I don't know," I answer.

"You haven't looked at the account since we set it up?" Amanda asks.

"I was going to but then got busy. Besides, I didn't want to know the results before Hunter."

"We?" Hunter asks Amanda. "You helped him?"

"Not really," she answers. "I knew he was doing it.

Remember that spitting contest we did?"

"Actually, we did several," Hunter reminds her.

"Yeah, well, that's how he got your DNA. After that I wasn't involved."

Amanda is making it sound like she's totally innocent.

Ignoring Amanda, I direct Hunter's attention to the screen. "A star in the corner of a specific person in your tree indicates there are records to look at to verify or deny. For you to determine if that person or information belongs on your tree."

"Records like what?" she asks.

"You honestly don't know anything about these ancestral websites?" Amanda asks.

Hunter shakes her head. "Not really."

"How can you be so unaware?" Amanda snorts.

"Too bad you aren't sometimes," I respond. "Not everyone needs to know everything. You're just annoyed you aren't connected to royalty." Amanda is obsessed with everything royal. Hunter couldn't care less. Hunter prefers learning about the historical laws and customs of a society. Amanda is all about family connections. Particularly with Queen Victoria and all her descendants.

I click on a question mark. The screen prompt is asking if we want to create a double family tree.

Hunter is staring at the screen. "Say yes," she breathes.

I do.

Instructions on how to add an adopted family tree appear.

"What the heck does that mean?" Amanda asks.

Hunter reveals no emotion as she scans through the instructions quickly. Faster than me, in fact.

She turns my laptop toward her and clicks the star on the first hidden picture, then the second one next to it. Two names appear. Quickly, she clicks on each one and begins building and adding relative connections.

I watch and notice Amanda is watching, too.

Hunter is a quick study. Especially when it comes to computer programs and how they operate, but she readily admits she tends to avoid new programs. She doesn't like how long it takes her to learn them, though she's learning this one fast.

There isn't anything she can't solve when it comes to any problem if she puts her mind to it. In class, her skills were amazing. It surprised me she lacked the passion to pursue computering. In school, Amanda was as good as I was, but of the three of us, Hunter would beat us at every task and had better grades, but that was the end of her interest. Even now, for her, computers are just a means to an end. For me, computers became the foundation of my career in IT for my day job, and a graphic designer on the side. I build websites too.

Finished, Hunter slides the computer back in front of me, so we can all see the screen again. "I'm adopted."

On the screen, the once solid lines of her parents are dotted, and the solid lines now belong to two different people who were never married. In that short time, she created a sizable tree with multiple layers. Obviously, connections already created by others. All she had to do was add them to her tree.

"That's impossible," Amanda cries out. "Your parents would have told you."

"Would they?" she asks.

"Sure, they would. They never kept anything from you," I say. "They talked with you about sex long before our parents did. Plus, they let you read anything you wanted with no restrictions. You had the best parents."

"Apparently, they didn't tell me this. They hid it well."

"Oh, my god, Hunter," Amanda says. "Look." She points up the line at the parents of the adopted parents. "There's another double tree. And there's a third one. That's insane."

"You've got a family tree of multiple adoptions?" I ask.

"Looks that way, doesn't it?"

And then, she drops the emotional bomb in a shaky voice that twists my heart.

"My happy childhood was a lie. My entire life is a lie."

Chapter 5

Amanda McFadden

Mars and I are able to talk Hunter into letting us drive her home. She rides in my car, and Mars drives Hunter's car home for her. The plan is for me to take Mars back to the deli so he can pick up his car.

Hunter says little other than to repeat how her life has been a lie and wonders what she should do next. I tell her not to do anything, that people make mistakes when they don't think things through and make decisions too quickly.

"Your parents loved you," I remind her.

"I know they did—even if they were misguided."

"Misguided how?"

"By not being honest."

"They must have had their reasons."

"Everyone has reasons for everything they do, don't they? Always rationalizing their behavior."

"Don't you?"

She doesn't answer. She knows the answer is yes. Haven't we commented often enough about how we rationalized our way through the last decade? Hers for being stood up at the altar and then breaking off a second engagement. Me for the way I've been consuming candy and hiding most of it. We all have our reasons. What they don't know is that I'm adopted, too. I never wanted anyone to know I was different from them. My parents told me when I was little. It never came up because we moved here from a western state right after I'd been adopted. No one knew us here, so it became a nonissue. It's hard not to share that information with Hunter now.

Unlike Hunter, I know all about my birth parents. I've seen pictures and know we were in a horrible accident that left me an orphan. I'm thankful I've always known about my background. If only they had been royal—but that's always been a secret fantasy.

I follow Mars into her driveway. The house where she grew up and still lives. It's too big of a house for one person, she claims, but she likes it. It's cozy and feels like home, despite her parents having been murdered during a robbery gone wrong just before we graduated from college.

Sometimes, I wonder if she's being honest with herself, but I don't want to ask. I don't want her sinking into a hole of depression. Of course, I wonder if it has to do with finances as to why she stays in the house. Another reason why I don't ask. While I enjoy digging into the lives of dead royals, I don't like digging through the lives of people I know and work with.

"Thanks for driving me home," she says, getting out and accepting her keys from Mars. They hug. "Thanks for the present," she tells him, then adds, "I think."

"See you tomorrow at the library," I say.

She nods and heads for the house.

We watch her climb the stairs, cross the porch, and insert a key into the door. Just before she disappears inside, she waves.

We wave back.

Mars slides in beside me. I put the car into reverse and begin backing out of the driveway.

"What do you think?" Mars asks.

"Considering the bombshell news she received, it went as well as could be expected."

"In Hunter fashion," he adds.

Chapter 6

Hunter

I'm at my desk a couple of hours before my shift begins the next day. It's Friday, and I want to be alone. Without Amanda. I want to access the library's ancestry archives. Access I don't have at home. As far as anyone else knows, I'm checking for a patron, not for myself. If Amanda were here, she'd know differently right away.

My cursor hovers over the name of Sawyer Van Houten, my great-grandfather, when I hear Amanda's voice.

I exit the program and stash my notes in a side drawer of my desk. I don't want her becoming concerned about me, nor do I relish rehashing last night.

I pick up the stack of books I placed on my desk earlier, so it looks like I've been busy working with them.

"Oh, hi," she says, seeing me come out of my cubicle. "I thought I saw your car in the parking lot. You're usually not in this early."

"Just wanted to get a start on a typical Friday," I answer. She knows what I mean since Friday can be jam-packed with activities and tasks.

An hour before my shift ends, the library director asks to talk to me privately. We go into the little room next to my office. There aren't many private spaces in the back. Even her desk is out in the open.

"I'm so sorry that I have to do this," she begins.

Then don't, I think to myself. Inwardly, I sigh. I know

what's coming. I'd seen it often enough over the past decade as local library tax millage proposals haven't passed and state budgets have been slashed. She's going to let me go. Of all the full-time staff here, I have the least seniority. By less than a week—just a few days because I took a side trip before coming home, choosing to drive home after college was over. Amanda flew home and was hired before me. She applied the same day she returned home from college.

"I have to let you go. I don't have a choice."

"The budget, I know."

"You're going to be my first rehire, I promise!" She hugs me, then tells me to take home anything that is mine. She lets me go to my desk unaccompanied. I've seen other folks when told they were fired being escorted to their desks and given only ten or fifteen minutes to collect their stuff. Most people getting fired are angry.

I'm not like most people. I observe the big picture—the circumstances—plus, I rarely react to changes. I learned to see the telltale signs that indicate change is on the horizon; that way I'm rarely surprised. How often has the director told me that's what she likes about me? I know it's why she's giving me this last hour alone. Besides, she wants me back. She won't jeopardize her ability to rehire me by making me feel crowded or rushed. She knows that about me, too. It's why I had come in early, so Amanda wouldn't crowd me.

By the time Amanda learns of my immediate non-future here, my belongings fill several boxes on my desk. She's been busy with after-school activities that took place on the other side of the floor and in one of the few closed rooms, allowing the kids to be noisy. Otherwise, she would have been here sooner. My early gathering of research material is tucked in a cloth zippered bag and in the car already.

"I can't believe they're letting you go!" She peers into the box on the edge of my desk.

"I can. We've talked about it often enough when it happened to others."

"What are you going to do?"

"Read, I think."

"No, you should travel! It's time to live your life instead of reading it."

"But I don't like to travel. I'm satisfied looking at the pictures. Besides, I can't afford it."

"But your folks—"

"Left me the house and some chump change for home repairs. Not the millions—okay thousands—I need if I want to travel."

"You could if you weren't squirreling away every nickel for that out-of-reach dream of yours."

Amanda thinks my desire to own a house like those I read about in Gothic novels is idiotic. She never says it like that in so many words, but I know it's what she thinks. It's one thing to own a small cottage with a few bedrooms and turn it into a bed-and-breakfast, but an enormous house with a few staff? She thinks I'm out of my mind. Actually, she told me that the first time I talked about owning a B&B, but she hasn't said anything since then. I guess my scowl was long-lasting.

Once my parents died, having left me the house, she suggested I turn it into a B&B. A pleasant idea but given the neighborhood is in an old Detroit suburb, close to nothing but other houses just like it, I can't see tourists wanting to stay there. Besides, while this house is too big for just me, it's too small for a bed-and-breakfast.

She continues. "Wouldn't you rather live an adventure like those Gothics you read?"

"No. I'm satisfied just reading about them. Besides, no one ever lives like that now."

"You mean like in *Jane Eyre, Rebecca,* and *My Cousin Rachel*?" she asks.

"I'd love a big house for the business but not one so dilapidated and dreary that it would better suit Dracula, vampires, or The Munsters. Why do you have to always pick on my favorite books?"

She ignores my question. "So, after you read a few new books, what are you going to do?"

"What everyone else would do. Find another job."

"Doing what?"

"I don't know."

Chapter 7

Hunter

At home, I shut the door behind me and drop the box in my arms by the front door. I'll get the other two boxes from the car in a minute.

I smile hearing toenails on the wooden floor. "Daisy!" I kneel and welcome my Highland terrier into my arms. Pure white except for a splash of pale-yellow fur on her back, she reminds me of a Shasta daisy with its yellow center. The only time I ever see her this excited is when I come home. However, there was that time when she had cornered a groundhog in the backyard, snarling and dancing around it.

I'd gotten her from the dog pound soon after my parents had died. We both needed some company and companionship.

"Thank goodness I have you to come home to, no matter how bad my day is." I hold her face between my hands. I swear she's human from the way her eyes move back and forth, watching mine as I talk. Her brows furrow, too. "I may have lost my job, but I'll never lose you!"

She licks my nose, and I kiss her head. "I'll be right back."

Immediately, Daisy turns and retreats to the kitchen where her downstairs bed is near the bay window, the only place where sunlight hits the floor.

Back outside, half my body is in the back seat of the car. One of the boxes tipped, spilling its contents onto the floor. I'm in the middle of retrieving everything, rather awkwardly I might add, when a car pulls up behind mine. I raise my head and peer through the back window.

Mars.

He trots toward me, throwing the toothpick that was in his mouth to the ground. He knows I think it's a disgusting habit, especially since he soaks them in whisky. I called it an oral fixation one time, and he became defensive. Never made that mistake again. I get out of the car to greet him. He gives me a big hug, and I ignore the littering.

"Amanda called you, didn't she?"

"Yes. I'm here to help."

"Seriously, Mars, there's nothing to do."

"I hate how everything is happening to you."

"So does Amanda, but you don't see her here."

"She's bringing pizza."

I groan. "Seriously, you guys. I'm okay. I'm a big girl. I'll manage."

"With our help. Now what can I do?"

Why not use him, I consider. I have all kinds of chores I've been putting off. "Can you finish getting all that stuff out of the backseat and into the house?"

"Sure thing."

Okay, I can use some of his enthusiasm, too. As he throws himself into the task, I smile. He always knows how to cheer me up. And, Amanda is sure to keep me moving forward. I can't ask for better friends.

Chapter 8

Hunter

Mars enters the house before me. Immediately, Daisy emerges from the kitchen, growling and barking at him, nipping at his shoes. He learned long ago not to come into my house barefoot, not if he wants to keep his toes intact.

"Daisy! Bed! Now!" I command.

She gives him one last growl while looking at me, turns, and trots back to her bed. I could have sworn her tail bristled in defiance. Almost as if she's giving Mars the finger.

Minutes later, Amanda arrives and calls to have pizza delivered, which is going to take an hour, being it's Friday night. Mars misunderstood Amanda bringing pizza versus calling for it once she got here. He does that a lot. Misunderstanding. Miscommunicating. A reason he avoids a romantic relationship with her? Despite that, he's always been her dream.

I tell them that while we wait, we can mow the backyard and weed Mom's flower beds. Because the beds are mulched in the spring and fall, there aren't many weeds, but better to get them now while I have help, than to struggle with it on my own over several weeks.

Amanda quickly calls dibs on the riding mower. Mars agrees to use the trimmer while I weed. He'll be done in mere minutes. Amanda will be done in about twenty minutes, and then they'll both be helping me tidy up the beds, weeding and deflowering dead heads.

As I pull weeds and toss them on the grass for Amanda to

mow over, Daisy grabs one and shakes her head back and forth as if she has caught something alive. Then, she drops it and quickly snags the next one I toss out, repeating the *kill* before releasing it.

By the time she's caught and killed a dozen weeds, she's done and retreats under a lawn chair, watching us work.

Mom had created beautiful flower beds that still circle the backyard. I couldn't let them go after she died. It keeps us connected. The flowers are gorgeous, and I often took an assortment of cut bouquets to the library throughout the summer for the front desk.

"Still going to supply the library with your arrangements?" Amanda asks, coming up beside me, wrapping an arm around my shoulders.

"Be silly not to. Mom liked having her flowers shared."

Minutes later we're in the house, cleaned up and hands washed, and sitting in the living room, awaiting the pizza.

When the doorbell rings, Amanda jumps up. "My turn."

Whenever we get together like this, we take turns paying. Amanda always knows whose turn it is. She's good with numbers, and both she and Mars have killer memory abilities. I can't remember anything.

Multiple footsteps sound in the entry. A man, holding a briefcase walks into the room, with Amanda following.

"Hunter, this is Drew Anderson—"

Mars interrupts. "With Walker and Walker."

How does Mars know that?

Drew nods. "I'm sorry for the interruption. I have some important news to share with you." He stares at me, then his gaze darts to the other two before returning to me.

I frown.

"Alone," he says.

"These are my best friends. They know everything about

me. I prefer they stay." Is this day ever going to end with its surprises? I don't want to send them away, like little kids being punished. They'd probably have their ears to the wall if I sent them into another room, anyway. That or they'll pester me after he leaves, so why not just let them hear what he has to say?

The way Drew looks at me, I get the impression this won't be good news.

"As you wish," he says. "May I sit down?"

"Oh, certainly," I gush. "I'm so sorry. Can we get you something to drink?"

"No, no. I'm fine. I don't expect to be here that long." He sits, placing his briefcase on the coffee table where Mars cleared a space for him, pushing my reading material to the side.

Addressing his briefcase, he snaps open the two clasps on opposite ends, lifts the middle clasp, then opens the lid with his right hand and reaches into it with his left. Pulling out a small pile of papers, he closes the lid, putting the papers on top of the briefcase.

Amanda, by now, has sunk into the matching cushioned chair opposite mine and across the coffee table. Mars sits next to Drew. I can tell Mars is quickly scanning the top sheet of paper. His eyes grow large. He glances at me, his mouth forming an "O."

It takes a lot to surprise him, and I can tell he's genuinely surprised.

Drew begins. "I have to tell you that I've never seen a trust like this before. I doubt I'll ever see another one like it again." The second sentence was said more to himself than to us.

He continues. "To make a long story short: you're the sole heiress of a small island in northern Lake Huron, called Harbor House Island, which comes with an ancestral home and money enough to restore the house should you choose. A milling operation in Sinclair that you own as well, which was started by your great-great-great-grandfather, is still in operation and why the trust is still sound. It provides a decent yearly income, but it does have some debt."

All I can do is blink and stare, feeling numb.

Amanda says it for me. "What?!?"

The surprised look on my friends' faces has to be the same as mine.

"That can't be," I say. "How is it even possible?"

"Believe it or not," Drew answers, "the law firm on Drummond Island that oversees this property discovered your existence via your DNA profile online. Your DNA reveal was the final puzzle piece they'd been looking for."

"My adoption made that difficult?" I ask.

"Only because it's been hidden all this time due to sealed records. Plus, there was a total of three adoptions. Yours, your biological mother's adoption, and her biological mother's adoption. When your great-grandmother was killed and her husband disappeared, a relative took the baby—your grandmother—but something happened to the family and there was no paper trail of where your grandmother was taken. Or by whom.

"With the popularity of DNA submissions providing more profiles, the Board of Directors decided to do another search. They've been doing these searches every few years once the internet became commonplace. These in-between adoptions muddied their ability to find you because your adoption had been closed. The others weren't. The DNA profile is what finalized our hunt. While the other profiles don't have DNA profiles, once we had your profile, we were able to connect the lineage because the police, and then the trust kept your great-grandmother's DNA on record."

He digs through his papers, pulls out a sheet, and hands it to me. "This is the value of your inherited property, broken down via the land and buildings, the business, and cash on hand."

I can't believe what I'm looking at. All total, I'm a multi-millionaire because of the properties, but only a small portion of that is in cash. If I were to sell the business and the island, along with the house, along with Mom & Dad's house, I could buy property in Detroit somewhere and start my B&B. At the same time, it doesn't feel right to sell the island house or its island.

"How hard would it be to sell the business?" I ask.

"Not too difficult, but I can tell you that it wouldn't be profitable. Right now, it has debts to pay off, and buyers would be offering rock-bottom prices because of it."

"What about the island?"

"If you got the right broker and right buyer, maybe, but the house could be a hindrance. You might want to go look at it all before you make any final decisions. Don't forget, too, that there could be some significant inheritance tax to pay."

He gives me a few more papers to look at. The last sheet needs my signature, stating that he's given me the papers we talked about. After his handshake, he gives me his card, telling me to call anytime if I have questions.

Mars walks him to the door and returns with pizza in hand. "You can get the next two," he tells Amanda.

We go into the kitchen and sit at the bay-window breakfast table. Centered in the middle is the pizza box. Amanda gets lemonade from the refrigerator and fills three glasses with ice. Mars grabs plates and silverware and brings them to the table.

I sit at the table, staring out the window, the papers still in my hand. Once they both sit down, I push the papers aside as they hand me my utensils, plate, and drink.

After we all take a slice and eat a couple bites in silence, Mars asks, "What are you going to do?"

I shake my head. “I don’t know. I’m torn between wanting to drive up there and examine everything like a young child coming downstairs for Christmas morning and wanting to stay here and sell everything up there sight unseen, and be happy with whatever I can get and move forward with my B&B.

“You should travel the world,” Amanda exclaims.

“You’re the one who wants to travel,” Mars counters.

“You know I have no desire to travel,” I remind her. I can’t figure out why it’s so hard for Amanda to understand why we aren’t alike in that way and why I have to keep reminding her. Truth be known, we aren’t alike in a lot of different ways. Movies, food, books, shopping, clothing, and even hobbies. She collects sea glass. I collect rocks. At least those hobbies provide some commonality we can pursue together whenever we’re on one of Michigan’s beaches.

“I wonder if Drew knows how your great-grandmother was killed,” Amanda asks.

“We can probably find out online somewhere,” Mars says.

Chapter 9

Anonymous

Finally, my plan is in motion. Some careful maneuvering is needed now. After waiting this long, I can't screw this up.

Chapter 10*

Margaret Sinclair

1910

Sinclair lumberyard, Sinclair, Michigan, Drummond Island, in northern Lake Huron.

"Marry me." Six years old, I push the hair out of my eyes and swipe at the mud on my face so I can see Johnny, my rescuer, better.

Ever since he arrived at Sinclair a year ago, he's been working at Grandfather's logging camp with Father. Anytime he's in town, I follow him around. Though younger than the other boys, he's taller, leaner, and scrappier. He's thirteen, with warm brown eyes and hair to match, dimples when he smiles, and my hero.

"You're not old enough, Meggie."

"No one calls me Meggie." It's the first time he's ever called me that. "My name is Margaret."

"You'll always be Meggie to me, and I'll always protect you."

He just saved me from the trio of eight-year-old boys who like to bully me when no one's around. This time, though, they got caught pushing me into the mud, face down. Looking up and seeing Johnny coming my way was enough to send them running—in the opposite direction.

Both Grandfather and Father have told me that I need to stand up to the bullies, but it's difficult when I'm half their size.

"Will I be old enough next year?"

"We'll see."

From behind us, Father calls out to Johnny. "You coming or not, Boy?" He has the team hitched to the trailer, which is loaded with men and a few teenagers that he's taking out to the logging camp a mile away.

Johnny is the youngest of them all and has become Father's shadow, his right-hand man. I heard Father tell Grandfather that.

"Coming!" Johnny yells over my head. To me, he says, "I'll see you later."

I turn and watch him run to the wagon and jump on. I wave and he waves back.

*****

That night, I overhear Johnny and Grandfather talking as I stand at the upstairs rail. Grandfather is angry and Johnny says, "Nothing is as it seems." Apparently, Grandfather doesn't like the response because his voice gets louder. I can't hear much after that as they move into a different part of the house—Grandfather's den.

The door shuts, muffling their words, but I can tell Grandfather is angry just from the tenor of his voice. At the same time, I know he's not really angry at Johnny.

He's used that voice with me before, always apologizing and saying he's not mad at me but mad at the situations I'm confronted with and his not being able to help me directly. "Hating that I have to watch life and the cruelty of others confronting you. I could interfere but that would make things worse," he told me. I wasn't sure how, so I didn't say anything.

That conversation occurred just before Johnny arrived. Since then, Grandfather's outbursts have increased, but I've noticed he always calms down after talking with Johnny.

So, why is he yelling at Johnny?

*****

The next day, from my bedroom window, I see Johnny exiting the porch, suitcase in hand.

I gasp.

He's leaving!?! No! Why?

I raise the window.

He stops and looks up at me. He waves, saying, "Take care of him."

I lift my hand. There's nothing I can say that will keep him here. It's Grandfather's doing.

I find Grandfather in his den, standing in the middle of the room, his hands in his pockets, staring at the floor.

"Why's Johnny leaving? Don't you like him anymore?"

He looks up. "I like him," he says gruffly. There's a catch in his voice. He stares at me, his lips thinning. "If only—"

"My mother hadn't abandoned us—Father and me, and Father actually cared about me."

He nods with a tear in his eye. He blinks and it's gone. "I won't always be here to help you. I can't take care of you properly."

"You're going to abandon me, too?"

His head jerks, and he stares hard at me. "I will never abandon you. I just can't teach you what you need to learn. Someone else is going to have to do that—but abandon you? *Never!*"

My lips sealed tight, I stare back, giving him the same determined look he's giving me. We're alike that way.

He's sending me away. I know it as sure as I'm standing here in front of him. There'll be no argument. His word is law. I don't like it a bit, and there's no persuading him otherwise.

I dig my toe into the rug. I'm not done wanting answers. Looking up, I steel myself for an answer I probably won't like.

"Why did you fire him?"

He's working his mouth…thinking. I'm guessing, but there's no way Johnny would have left on his own. I know I'm guessing, but I can't believe Johnny would leave on his own, so I remain silent. I know if I wait long enough, he'll talk.

"He's been accused of stealing." His voice hardens. "He wouldn't tell me who the actual thief is. I gave him another chance this morning to come clean, but he wouldn't say."

"Someone you'd like to fire?"

"Yes."

"Why won't he tell, then?"

"I don't know. He's protecting someone."

"You?"

Surprised, he frowns, and sighs. "You're too smart for your own good."

"Is that when he said *Nothing is as it seems*?"

Grandfather studies me. "You listened?"

I nod, looking up at this old man I love, but not understanding why he's scowling at me. I know that face. I've seen it directed at Father and other men often enough to know that no one dares utter another word after that. His scowl never stopped me, though.

"He isn't coming back, is he?"

Silence.

"Because you can't let him back."

Grandfather nods his head slightly, his shoulders hunched in resignation.

I go up to him and hug him tight. He pats the top of my head, his face still lined with worry.

"Get on with you now."

He turns, facing the window. "Go ask the cook—" His voice cracks. "—when lunch will be ready."

I leave, shutting the door behind me. Even though I've been abandoned before by people who supposedly loved me, for the first time, I feel alone and deserted.

I look out the front door, which is open to the cool summer breeze. The door Johnny just stepped through before disappearing for good.

"I'll never forget you," I whisper. In that moment, I know he'll be the standard I'll measure everyone else against.

While I had shared everything with him, I know next to nothing about him. Other than his exceptional sense of honor.

*****

Three weeks later, I'm shipped off to a Detroit boarding school. Grandfather is paying a logger who broke his leg and is returning home to Detroit to escort me safely to the school.

Grandfather wants me to be brought up like a lady. Sinclair is tiny with only a few women and no girls. At the most northeastern part of Drummond Island with only a general store and a structure that serves as a hospital when needed or as a bunkhouse when the loggers stay in town.

Grandfather stands on the dock and watches me leave. I wave, and he takes his hand out of his pocket and starts to hold up his hand but stops midway. It's a half-wave. He's as torn up as I am.

My life is never going to be the same again.

Chapter 11*

Margaret

The school is a huge, gigantic brick building with a wide front porch with a swing and chairs. I've never seen anything so big. All the buildings in Detroit are big. And, the streets so busy. Filled with horses and buggies and horseless carriages.

The noise is deafening.

I stand on the sidewalk leading up to the steps with my one suitcase. After taking in the school, I turn to take in everything else: the people, the sidewalks, and streets filled with bicycles, cars, and buggies.

"Mary!"

A hand touches my shoulder.

"What are you doing out here—"

I turn toward the voice. An older girl with a surprised look on her face stares at me.

"You're not Mary."

"I'm Margaret Sinclair. Who are you?"

"Hildy Green." She takes my hand and my suitcase and pulls me up the stairs and into the school. "You've got to see this!" She continues pulling me along, going up another flight of stairs and down the hall where she opens the door to a room where a girl my height stands next to her bed. "Mary, look what I found. Your roommate and your twin."

The girl turns and I'm looking at myself. I'm speechless, but she's not. Immediately, she laughs, steps toward me, takes my hand, and pulls me into the room. She takes the bag from Hildy and lays it on the bed in the unoccupied half of the room. "We're going to be best friends! I'm Mary Corrigan."

As I unpack my bag, Mary chatters away, telling me all of the adventures we're going to have. Our birthdays are only days apart, and I discover she's everything I'm not. She laughs easily, is a prankster judging by the stories she's telling me, and appears to be friends with everyone considering how many people stop by to say hello.

I've never seen anyone talk so much or so fast!

Every time I look at Mary, I think I'm looking into a mirror.

I stash my empty suitcase under the bed, straighten, and turn around to see Mary at the mirror with scissors in her one hand and hair pulled away from her head in her other hand.

"What are you doing?!"

She has lovely long hair, while mine is cut in a bob.

"Fixing it so we look exactly alike. It'll grow out and so will yours."

Hair falls to the floor. I've never had long hair. I kind of like the idea of growing it out. It's always been short. Manageable, Grandfather would say.

I watch, not saying anything.

When finished, Mary pulls me over to the mirror and puts her arm around my shoulders. We stare at the image of two looking like one. Just as Hildy said, we're twins. In looks anyway. Same height, same skin tone, same build, and same hair coloring. And now, same hair length.

"This is going to be so much fun," she announces.

Chapter 12*

Margaret

1922, April

Over time, I watched how the other girls lapped up Mary's shenanigans and stories, and how teachers loved and forgave her despite her tricks and slacking off on her homework. She would have been an A student if she had done her homework. She's so smart, she rarely has to study, and yet, still aces all of her tests. At least those she takes. Well, half of them anyway.

I have to study all the time to get A's.

She offered to take my French exam for me once, but I said no. I wanted my grades to be my own even if they are only B's.

We've been mistaken for each other constantly, and Mary delights in dressing like me and doing her hair like mine. She laughs when the teachers mix us up, calling us by each other's names. I find it disrespectful. Now that I know her, I don't think we're *that* much alike. Mary has a smattering of freckles across her nose that she keeps hidden with makeup, saying it's the only mark of her Irish inheritance, unlike her siblings and parents who are all redheads. When they come to visit, even they mix us up when seeing us from behind or from a distance.

Mary's hair has a red tint, while my hair is a mousy brown. Lackluster except in the summer when the sun lightens it a bit.

I've been here for twelve years, and now it's April 1922, my senior year. A wealthy matriarch sponsors the senior girls' coming out with an annual ball in her huge Detroit home every spring, which takes place later tonight.

I'm sitting on the porch swing, watching Mary entertain those around her with stories of her brothers. My birthday was yesterday, and Mary's was the day before.

Grandfather will be here, as will be her brothers.

I can't wait to see Grandfather. He's taking me to lunch and then to the ball later. It was hard leaving Grandfather back then, but Mary quickly filled the void.

We became best friends just as she predicted. She never shared anything I told her. And, she was always there comforting me whenever I missed Grandfather. I learned I could trust her.

Little by little she won me over, even to the point where I participated in a swap, but only because she was so sick. I felt sorry for her.

Pretending to be her, I was supposed to meet a new fella, a friend of her brothers, at a dance. Fortunately for me, he never showed up. I was so nervous, I vowed to never take her place ever again. I never told her that, but I always said *no* any time she asked. She called me a prude every time, but I didn't care. At least not that she knew.

Johnny's honor was always at the back of my mind.

I leave the front porch to change my clothes. It's time to get ready. Grandfather will be here any minute. As I change, I realize that when Mary leaves my life, Grandfather will be back in it again.

Despite everything, I will miss Mary. She brought joy and laughter into my life. Laughter that had been missing in Sinclair.

Chapter 13*

Margaret

I come downstairs and find Grandfather is already here and chatting with Mary.

It's the first time he's ever met her. No doubt, she introduced herself once she found out who he was.

At the Italian restaurant Grandfather picked out, he pulls out my chair and seats me, walks around the table, sits, and picks up his menu. His hand shakes a little. He looks older and moves a bit slower.

Immediately, he puts the menu down. "Can't wait to have a nice Italian meal. All I get at home is German cooking. Not that it's bad, mind you, but she can't seem to make a good spaghetti sauce."

"Well, it's probably tastier than anything I could cook because I don't know how to cook at all."

"They didn't teach cooking as a class?"

I shake my head.

"Sounds like your roommate, Mary, knows how to cook though. Says her family is Italian."

I nod my head. "On her father's side. Her mother's is Irish."

"You should bring her home with you this summer. Let her teach you how to cook."

"Seriously?"

A waiter asks if we're ready to order. Grandfather asks if there's any chance of getting some bourbon.

The waiter laughs. "You and every other customer."

"Damn prohibition," Grandfather complains. "Can't wait until it's over with."

Our orders taken, the waiter leaves.

"So, what would you like as a graduation present?" he asks, sliding over a small package. "Besides this."

"Nothing," I respond, picking it up. I open it to find a small bottle of eau de parfum with a lilac flower on the glass.

"It was your grandmother's favorite."

"Thank you. I'm thrilled that you want to introduce me at the ball and be my first dance partner." I pick up my water glass and hold it up to him. "Despite this being one of your busiest times?"

Grandfather lifts his glass and clinks it with mine, takes a swallow and returns the glass to the table. "That should be booze. Somehow, your dad is able to get me a bottle now and then. He has no idea how to run the business." He shakes his head. He sits back and stares at me. "Surely, there's something else that you want."

"Only to come home again."

"Done. Anything else?"

"Not really."

"How about ownership of Harbor House Island and the house?"

My jaw drops, and he leans forward, reaching across the table, chucking me under my chin, closing my mouth the way he used to do when I was little.

He grins. "I'm happy you're surprised."

He knows how much I love Harbor House Island and the house. I've only been inside it once. Once was all it took for me to fall in love with the large rooms and the view from the sole turret, Grandmother's bedroom. I don't remember who took me there or for what reason, but the memory of the house has stayed with me. "Can I live in it right away?"

Grandfather built the house for Grandmother but deserted it and the island after Grandmother died shortly before I was born.

"Given no one has for nearly two decades? Probably not. At least, not right away. I'll have to hire a carpenter or someone who can do repairs and restoration work. Might be a good idea to find someone while I'm down here. Frank might know of someone."

"Frank?"

"Frank Darnell. He's the branch manager of the bank in Sinclair."

"Sinclair is all that now?"

He nods. "It's a bigger village now."

"Won't Father be upset that you're giving me the island and the house?"

Immediately, there's a scowl on his face. "He doesn't deserve it." His face softens a little, turning sad, then angry, then sad again. Something has happened between them. Neither has ever spoken of any strife in their letters, scarce as they were. Nor did Grandfather say anything when he was here two years ago either. Though at the time, I learned Father had been to Detroit several times that year, but not once did he visit me. Did he not want me to know he was in town? It just reinforced my earliest belief that he didn't care much about me.

"Your Grandmother knew your father never wanted to stay in Sinclair. Besides, I've always known you wanted to live in the house—"

"And, use her bedroom as mine?"

He nods. "If that's what you want." He pulls out his watch. "Time to go and prepare for your big event."

"Were you serious about my inviting Mary to Sinclair for summer?"

"Only if she can teach you how to make spaghetti sauce."

I grin. "Deal."

I'll have *both* Grandfather and Mary with me. No doubt, she'll be excited to learn she doesn't have to go home for a few months.

Chapter 14

Hunter

Present Day

Two days later, I meet Mars and Amanda at the deli for dinner and am the first to arrive at our usual booth. Over pizza two nights ago after Drew left, I told them I was going to do some heavy thinking.

I don't relish being a property owner in two locations that are over 300 miles apart. I'm not hoity-toity enough. Let alone rich enough. Amanda, though, could do it. She'd make it happen somehow.

Waiting for our meals to be brought to our table, I tell them I stopped at Drew's office.

Mars hands me a copy of an old newspaper report about Margaret Sinclair. That she had been murdered, her husband was missing, and that their baby had been in the other room unharmed. Nothing more.

"She was engaged to one man but married another," I inject.

Both stare at me.

"It's quite the story according to Drew," I say. "My great-grandmother was given the island and the house when she became engaged to Frank Darnell but lived there with Sawyer, instead, after their marriage."

I tell them how my three-time great-grandfather George Sinclair founded Sinclair, a village on Drummond Island after the Civil War and had made his fortune with his mill and Michigan's northern forests. How he built Harbor House on a small island nearby and that his only son—Margaret's father—Edward (Eddie) Sinclair had died while jailed in Detroit, a victim of the Spanish flu outbreak.

"Jailed for what?" Amanda asks.

"Bootlegging," I say.

I reach into my bag. "He gave me this with some papers."

I put a small, handmade wooden box in the middle of the table. On the lid is an engraved owl with outstretched wings. "It was part of Margaret's possessions."

Amanda fingers the owl. "Wow, this carving is exquisite."

Mars picks up the box and turns it this way and that. "What kind of papers? Do you have a key for this?" He holds the box up close, studying the lock on it.

"No key," I say. "He gave me the deed to the island and house. Some papers that dealt with the business. All current legal stuff."

"Do you want it opened?" he asks, indicating the box.

I nod.

Mars says, "That isn't an ordinary lock." Holding the box with one hand, he digs into his pocket with the other. He pulls out a key ring that contains mostly Allen wrenches, but some have different shaped tips. He sees me staring at the keys. "For using on small computer screws," he tells me. Makes sense with his IT job. He repairs computers on the side when he's not creating graphics or websites for customers.

A first for me. Seeing him at work, analyzing a lock. I've seen him analyzing computer innards lots of times, but never a lock.

He selects a tool and slides it into the keyhole, then holds the box up to his ear while he twists the tool a little. The lid pops open. "Voila!"

"That's amazing," Amanda coos.

He hands me the box. Inside is a bit of hair tied with a slim pink ribbon, made into a bow, and a key. I pick up the key and palm it.

Mars picks it out of my hand, inspecting it. "It's tiny. Not a normal key."

Amanda takes it from him. "It's funny that you weren't given a key to the box but there's one inside instead." She hands it back to me.

"I don't get it either. It almost looks like it would fit the box."

Amanda claps her hands. "Isn't this exciting? You could be living the life of one of your heroines. In search of a door that fits this key."

"Let's try it." Mars shuts the lid and inserts the key into the lock. He turns the key. Nothing.

Mars pulls the key out of the lock, handing it to me. "It looks like one of those keys my sisters used to have for their diaries."

"I'm inclined just to sell everything sight unseen," I say.

"Oh, no, you can't do that," Mars insists excitedly. "You should at least take a look at the place."

Amanda nods. "Yes, do it!"

"I don't know if I have time," I say. "I need to look for another job."

"If it makes your decision any easier, I'll go with you," Mars says.

I smile at him. So, like him, to want to make it easier for me or Amanda. He's a generous man, always offering help to anyone who asks for it. Trouble is, I'm not asking.

"Me, too," Amanda says. "I'm ready for a vacation."

They're going to insist.

She grabs my hand. "It wouldn't be the same if you were doing this on your own and we weren't together."

I appreciate their willingness to accompany me. *If* I go, do I want their company? As much as I want to go alone, with the three of us, we could get a lot done quickly. I don't want them to think I'm eager for their company, though, so I let them dangle on the hook by saying, "I need to think about it. I'll let you know when I've decided."

From time to time, I've had to use boundaries. Sometimes it's fun watching how much they want to do something with me, and sometimes I'd take a day or two to think about it before saying *yes*. Amanda, especially, hates it. She likes to make snappy decisions. Mars does too. I'm the one who takes forever to decide anything. The only reason I ended up in a computer class with them was because Mars took the pen out of my hand as I contemplated which electives to take and filled in one slot for me.

Amanda squeezes my hand and releases it, and Mars nods.

He shoulders his bag. "I'd love to stay, but I'm meeting a new client. Always someone needing help with their computer."

Amanda and I gather our stuff and leave with him.

Not wanting to rehash everything again, I'm glad to be going home. I need alone time with Daisy to think about my options.

Stepping out onto the sidewalk, we all look up at the sky that has turned an ugly gray-green color.

"Looks like a huge storm," Amanda says.

"It's been crawling across the state all day long," Mars says. "Slow moving."

"Stay safe," I tell them, heading for my car.

Chapter 15

Hunter

Driving home, I can't help but think about the past few days' events. I need to make a decision, and the sooner I do it the better.

Once home, I feed Daisy. Looking out the window, I notice the wind picks up. I go back outside and drive the car into the unattached garage that sits further back on the property. Dad had built a screened porch, attaching it to the garage. We called it our outdoor porch. A successful way of avoiding mosquito bites.

Between the porch and the house, he and Mom had created a large stone walkway, with an immense flower garden circling the yard. Grass grows on both sides of the walk, and the grass rarely burns in the scorching summer sun because the immense tree behind the garage shades much of it.

Before shutting the garage door, I retrieve the now empty garbage can from the curb and roll it into the garage. Normally, it's stored outside, on the other side of the garage, out of sight when looking out the kitchen window.

Inside, checking the weather channel, I see the storm's intensity is huge. A tornado watch is in effect. High winds and rain for sure.

Back outside and in the backyard, I put flower pots inside the screened porch, and tuck the chairs around the table, collapsing the umbrella and tying it down properly. I start to walk away but reconsider the umbrella and go back, removing it instead. I carry it into the outdoor porch, placing it on the floor, alongside a screened wall. I end up propping open the door, bringing in the chairs, too. The table, though, I have to leave outside. It's just too big to get through the door and too heavy for me to deal with.

Big drops of rain fall as I return to the house. I scamper inside just in time, missing the deluge of rain.

I pour a glass of iced tea and move into the living room to sit by the huge front window to watch the storm. I grab a legal pad of yellow paper and a pencil.

The room darkens, so I turn on a soft light in the corner. Normally, once I turn on the lights, I shut the curtains, but this time I leave them open. I'm not ready to shut out a view of the storm.

Settled in the chair, I sip the tea and draw a line down the middle of the top sheet of paper. Writing *Pro* on one side and *Con* on the other, I record good reasons for traveling to Sinclair and inspecting the place, and on the opposite side, reasons why doing so isn't worth my time.

Even though Amanda always makes fun of my pro-and-con sheets, I want to have evidence of my decision should she ask. Basically, I have a sound idea of what I want to do, but going through this exercise helps solidify my decision.

For an hour, the wind gusts, whipping treetops in circles. I've never seen this much rain in such a short time. The news channel warns of flooding in parts of the city, stating which areas to avoid.

By the time the storm has abated, water drips from the eaves, and the wind is nonexistent. The storm had been noisy as it roared through the community. Now, everything is quiet. Even Daisy, who had crawled onto my lap shivering in fear, lies tucked up against the arm of the chair and my leg, sleeping peacefully.

I look at the sheet's two columns and see they're nearly equal in length. It has me rethinking my earlier decision to go.

Maybe I'll wake up in the morning knowing what I should do.

I finish the tea, hold the glass in one hand, and pick up Daisy with the other, tucking her under my arm. In the kitchen, I deposit the glass in the sink and turn off lights as I move back to the front of the house to close the front curtains.

Sleeping on my decision sounds like a good plan. Just as I'm about to go up the stairs, I have a thought.

I put Daisy on the floor, and she scampers to the kitchen. Probably for some water.

I go to the pad of paper and flip the page. This time, I head the page with a question: *What do you lose if you go / don't go?* Quickly, I jot down my thoughts. There are more benefits in not going. Time. Expense. Dealing with unknowns that others better suited can deal with. Plus, I'll be able to search for a new job now and not have to wait until I return. A reasonable decision.

Daisy returns from the kitchen and gives me her *I need to go outside* whine. I walk back into the kitchen with her, and without turning on the light so it wouldn't attract bugs, I open the door. She scoots out quickly.

A minute later, she's back inside. I don't blame her for not wanting to stay out any longer than she has to, since it's still drizzling out.

She stands at the door, waiting for me to wipe her wet paws dry.

CRACK!

Startled, I stand, looking out.

I can't see anything.

Another huge CRACK.

The ground and the house shake.

I turn on the outside lights.

Leaves and tree limbs are on the ground where the patio table should have been, with more leaves and limbs disappearing into the darkness.

The monster tree came down!

I grab a heavy-duty flashlight, put on my shoes, and step outside.

I can't see the outdoor porch or the garage.

Following the back wall of the house, I go out to the driveway, which is clear, then point the flashlight beam at the garage. While the garage door is clear, the roof isn't.

The enormous trunk of the tree has split the building in half. Heavy limbs demolished the outdoor porch. No doubt my car is crushed as it sits in the garage.

I can't be without a car! How will I go looking for another job?

My thoughts spin.

Going back inside, I go straight to the phone and call my insurance agent, Richard. I'm forced to leave a message, no doubt because it's so late.

Ten minutes later, I'm surprised when he returns the call, saying he expected there'd be customers affected by the storm, so he went to the office.

Minutes later, I hang up, feeling better. He assured me I'll be given a loaner tomorrow and that he'll be out to assess the damage.

Even though he told me not to worry, as I prepare for bed, I don't think I'll be able to sleep.

Sure enough, sleep is slow in coming. My dreams are filled with multiple storms.

Chapter 16

Hunter

By mid-afternoon, Richard is true to his word. He just delivered a loaner car and is assessing the damage.

"Are you aware that the porch isn't covered and that you have a sizeable deductible?" he asks.

I stare at him. "What?" In the morning light, it was disappointing to discover the screened porch totally destroyed along with the garage. Now, I learn it's not covered at all.

"Your dad never updated his policy to cover the porch."

"He'd finished it shortly before he was killed."

Richard nods. "And, the last time we had talked, he'd told me that he wanted to reduce the deductible but hadn't. Plus, the coverage you do have covers its original value—not what it would cost to rebuild it at today's prices."

This time I nod, saying, "And, when you talked with me after their deaths, I didn't follow up."

"It was overwhelming, I'm sure."

"So, give me the bad news. What do you estimate as the cost for repairs?"

The more he talks, the more distant I become. It feels like being told Mom and Dad have been murdered in a robbery all over again.

It happened as they sat around the fire pit in the backyard. A robber who had come in the front door, and left via the back door, not realizing they were in the backyard. Shot them both. Execution style. A bullet each to the head.

Since then, I removed the pit, replacing it with a birdbath, surrounding it with flowers. Mom would have liked that.

My car, which isn't even a year old, will pay out enough so I can at least buy a compact car. Though, it may have to be a used car this time. I can't get a loan without a job, so I doubt I can afford to buy a new one. I don't trust having the money Drew told me I have, nor do I want to spend my savings on a new car. Used is good enough.

As it turns out, the damage to the garage and porch is total, and the insurance company won't cover rebuilding costs. Considering the house and the garage are 75 years old, I can't afford to rebuild. My savings could cover having the tree removed and demolishing the garage, but I'd use up everything I have, emptying my savings account. I need that savings to live on while I look for another job.

I don't know what I'm doing with the inherited property or the business. I have no idea how much of my inherited cash will be needed to deal with that property.

I don't have a choice.

I need to sell this house. As is.

And, go up and decide what to do with that property.

Mars and Amanda are going to think I'm insane.

Chapter 17

Hunter

The next day, I invite Mars and Amanda over for dinner.

I sit on the porch glider, waiting and watching for them to arrive.

True to form, they arrive together. No doubt Amanda called Mars and asked if he'd pick her up.

They can't stop staring at the treed garage and the destruction as they get out of the car. They stand rooted in place. I step off the porch to join them.

"Oh, that's bad." Amanda hugs me. "I'd still be crying if that was my house."

Mars laughs. "You rent."

"Still, you know what I mean."

I tell her I know what she means.

Mars gives me a big hug and an extra squeeze at the end. "I'm so sorry. I know how much you loved that backyard porch. At least, you can rebuild."

Standing between the two of them, I slide my hands through their arms and crook my arms, which they imitate. "Actually, I can't."

Three across and in unison, we step across the yard to the porch. They both respond at the same time.

"Wait, what?"

"Yes, you can."

Typical of Mars wanting more information and Amanda already telling me what I should do.

"Come inside. I made lasagna. I'll tell you all about it."

Minutes later, plates full and water glasses filled, we sit in the breakfast nook and look at the tree's top as it lies on the ground through the window.

"That's so sad," Mars says of the tree. "It's like looking at a corpse."

"That morose," Amanda says.

"But fact," I say. I'm done dealing with the emotional pain of it all. I'm ready to move on. I'd like them on board with my plan. If not, I'm prepared to go alone. "I've decided to sell this place and go up north."

"Sell *this* place?" Mars looks stricken. "But, it's your family home."

"*Was* my family. My adopted family. It's not my true family home." I pick up my water and down half the glass.

Amanda's loaded fork stops mid-air. "Wow, so you're going to brush them aside, just like that?"

I set my glass down, cupping my fingers around the glass, and slide my fingers down toward the coaster. "Not any more than they brushed my feelings aside by not being honest with me."

Amanda lowers her fork. "That's harsh, even for you. They loved you."

"But not enough to be honest with me."

Mars says, "Maybe they were scared you'd reject them—"

Amanda didn't let him finish. "Like you're doing to them now."

I stare at Amanda, grit my teeth, then ask quietly, without emotion. "What do you know about it? Anything?"

Her eyes widen in surprise. Her head and torso shrink backward into the chair. "No, noth...Nothing."

I inhale deeply and exhale, blowing out purposefully.

Something I do when stressed. Usually alone in my room or a bathroom stall. I'm good at hiding my stress. People have no idea how my calm exterior camouflages warlike seething rage or disgust at events or other people. Right now, I'm trying to squelch down both the events of the past few days and the obstacles they're presenting.

I don't need my two best friends to be part of that resistance.

Earlier, I had prepared myself to cut them out of my plan if needed for the sake of sanity, but I love them dearly, even if they annoy me at times. It's always been like that. I want to include them, but I don't want to keep explaining myself either.

Nor do I want to be totally alone, abandoned just because we don't agree at the moment. They have no clue how I've changed since learning I was adopted, then having to deal with my parents' deaths and now all of this.

Because of the story, my determination is stronger and a priority right now.

"What I'm about to tell you isn't up for discussion. It is what it is, and I'm not changing my mind. I've thought long and hard about it. I don't have the money to make the repairs here. I'm selling it as is."

"The tree forced your hand," Mars comments.

Finally. Some support. "It did. And, it's been a relief knowing that I won't have to deal with this disaster."

"How so?" he asks.

"I've known for some time this place is too big for me—"

"But, isn't the house up north even bigger?" Amanda asks.

"Definitely. But, it's perfect for a B&B."

"As far as you—," Mars inserts.

"Yes," I interrupt quickly.

"You're really going through with your B&B plan?" Amanda asks.

"I am. I don't know what will happen once I get there, if it'll be too much or worth doing, but that's my plan, right now."

With Mars, there's always an *and* or a *but.* He's a critical thinker and, no doubt, already ahead of me.

"And—?"

There it is. I jump in. "And, if it isn't what I think it should be, I'll be selling everything up there and finding a place that I *can* turn into a B&B. At the very least, we'll have a fun vacation up north."

"We?" Amanda asks.

"Since you both expressed wanting to come with me, I'm inviting you both to do so." I know it wouldn't be a problem for Mars since he works out of his house and can bring his laptop with him, but I know Amanda will have to use her vacation days. I also know she has more than enough vacation days saved up, probably twice the number she'd be gone.

Amanda claps her hands. "Yes!"

"But, you haven't even asked your supervisor," Mars says.

"Not a problem," she says.

Her answer surprises me. Usually, we had to give the director advance notice a couple weeks ahead of time.

"When do we leave?" she asks.

"In three days. The house is going on the market at the end of the week, and I'm spending the next few days selling furniture and anything else I don't want to keep, storing what I don't sell, and packing up everything else. I probably won't take much up with me. Essentials only."

"Need any help?" Mars offers.

"I'd love it."

"I would if I could, but I doubt—"

"Don't worry, Amanda. I get it. I know you'd like to help me pack, but work comes first."

She nods.

Work didn't come first. Her own desires did. She's coming because of Mars.

I stand and collect our plates. "So, who's ready for some Boston creme pie? Store-bought." Even though I know they love my home-baked pies, I can't let them think I made this one.

They spend the rest of the evening asking me an assortment of questions. Which pieces of furniture am I keeping? Where will I live if I come back? Mars asks if I'm taking Daisy. Hearing her name, she trots from her bed, growling as she passes Mars on her way to my chair and sits. I reach down and pet her.

"I am," I state.

He doesn't hide his disappointment very well.

I ignore him. "I don't know how long I'm going to be gone. I won't board her for several weeks. I don't understand why she dislikes you so much."

"Wish you'd find out," he mutters.

Amanda laughs. "Oh, you like the attention. It makes you special."

His face lights up as if suddenly he's in the spotlight. "Well, there is that."

For the first time in a long time, I'm excited. A new adventure. How long has it been since I was this eager? I'm due for a fun stretch of adventure.

The worst that can happen is finding I shouldn't have gone and sold it all sight unseen.

It can't get any worse than that, right?

Chapter 18

Anonymous

I couldn't have planned this any better. We're going to Harbor House Island. Where I will exact my revenge and make things happen.

Chapter 19*

Margaret

1922

At the ball, three of Mary's four older brothers are in attendance, and each claims a spot on my dance card. The fourth brother, the one next to her in age and whom I've met before, is in jail for bootlegging.

Mary, along with some of the other girls, associates these bootleggers with cowboys of the Wild West, all characters we've been reading about in dime novels. I hope her brother won't be leading a life of crime. Nothing good can come from it.

I know, too, how grateful she was for school, as it got her away from helping her mother manage the household and the younger children. Mary confided early in our relationship that when she first arrived, she had three younger siblings at home, but there have been more births in her family in the last ten years.

Mary bragged about how she was an expert at running a household—even at six years old—and then proved it during our stay here, taking charge of kitchen duties when the cooks were gone. And, when we had cleaning duties, she was the one who showed us tips on how to get the rooms cleaned quickly.

She boasted that one day she'd be running her own household, but she intended to marry rich instead of poor like so many of the women in her family did.

Mary's brothers are charming and excellent dance partners, but it's their friend who I find looking my way every time I dare peek at him.

The air vibrates as he steps our way. It's like watching the parting of the Red Sea as people step aside and out of his way.

His stare is intense, not taking his gaze off me once. Is he even blinking? His aura is commanding, and he's the most handsome of all the men here tonight. I'm not the only one peeking glances. With dark hair and an equally dark mustache and well-trimmed beard, he looks like royalty. He's taller than average and stands erect as if he owns the room. Even from a distance, I could tell his eyes were brown, but up close, they're mesmerizing.

For a brief second, I wonder if we've met before. Then, Mary is there, looping her arm around his elbow, forcing him to crook his arm as if escorting her, and introduces him as Mr. Frank Darnell.

"The banker from Sinclair?" I ask, surprised.

"One and the same," he replies. "I traveled with your grandfather. I'm here on business and to see family."

I wonder why Grandfather didn't tell me he came down with Mr. Darnell.

He asks me to dance. Not waiting for an answer, he takes my hand, leading the way to the dance floor, turns, and places his other hand on my back. He squeezes my hand lightly. I look up, confronted by his gaze.

That initial sizzle I felt before is gone. Now, I'm curious but cautious.

I ask a few questions, wanting to know more about this man who traveled with my grandfather. The more we talk, the softer his gaze, the tighter our dance embrace, even if ever so slightly. I can't step back even if I wanted to.

"Mr. Darnell—"

"Please, call me Frank."

"Frank," I smile. "How long have you been living in Sinclair?"

"Two years. I've been to the logging camp several times, but I've yet to tour Harbor House Island."

"You want to?"

"Very much. Your Father talks about it."

I'm surprised. "He was raised there. Grandmother died just before I was born."

"Yes, he's mentioned that."

"The island is tiny compared to its island neighbors." Then, in my excitement, I gush, "Grandfather is giving me Harbor House and the island as a graduation present." Immediately, I regret blurting that out, especially if Father hasn't been informed yet.

"You are? That's quite a gift. What are you going to do with it?"

"Live there, even though no one has for twenty years or so."

"I imagine you'll need a carpenter—"

"Yes, Grandfather said the same thing and is going to look for—"

"I know just the man. He's from here and quite the craftsman. He's been working for me for a while now. I'll talk to your grandfather for you."

Why is Frank being so thoughtful? Or is that him being a typical businessman, a banker? Thinking about future business? Remodeling a big house like that could become expensive. Is he thinking I'll need a loan? I know Grandfather wouldn't give it to me without financing the remodeling, but Frank wouldn't know that.

We chat through the entire dance, and I learn he'll be in Sinclair when I return home at the end of May.

The dance ends, and he returns me to the fringe of the dance floor, kisses my hand, bows, then walks to the other side of the room.

Suddenly, Mary is at my side, grabbing my arm. “Isn’t he dreamy?”

I watch as he and one of her brothers disappear through a doorway and nod. “Yes, he certainly is that,” I admit.

Chapter 20*

Margaret

I'm surprised the next evening when told I have a visitor downstairs. I walk into the receiving room and find Mary there with Frank leaning down, their heads together. Hearing my footsteps, they turn in unison. Frank straightens, steps back, and smiles brightly.

"Margaret," Mary said. "Guess who's taking us out to dinner?"

"And, for no apparent reason," Frank adds. "I just wanted to see you again. Though, I'll admit, it was Mary's idea."

She glances at him with a surprised look. Had I not been looking at her, I would have missed it, but then, she smiles at me and nods her head. "I did. I just didn't think he'd tell you that." She punches him lightly in the arm teasingly. "He's always one for surprises. Just like my brothers."

Over dinner, I discover that the two of them have known each other for some time. Frank ran around with her brothers.

"Mostly my oldest brother," Mary said. "Both he and Frank are eleven years older than me."

Watching them interact, I wonder if that's what it's like having siblings, an older brother.

*****

For the next few weeks, Frank visits every night, just sitting on the porch visiting. Sometimes Mary joins us.

Tonight, Frank is taking me out to dinner. Just me. Mary sends us off, saying we'll have cake to celebrate when we return.

"Celebrate? What are we celebrating?

"My going home with you for the summer!"

Frank looks surprised and glances at Mary. "You are?"

She smiles at him. Then, he's asking me, "When was this arranged?"

"The day of the ball," I respond. "But Grandfather wanted me to wait before inviting her."

"She told me just today! Isn't it wonderful?"

"I had no idea," he says. Why does he appear unsettled?

Mary goes to him and tucks her arm through his, a move I recognize as habit. I saw her doing it with her brothers at the ball, too. It's part of her charm.

She looks up at him, smiling. "This way, I won't be completely without family."

His eyebrows go up.

Quickly, he turns to me. "Are you ready to go?"

*****

We arrive at a fancy French restaurant, where we're seated at a table with a sizable bouquet. Flowers that other tables don't have. The waiter serves us without ever asking us what we want. Frank thanks him.

"Did you plan this?"

He reaches across the table and takes my hand. "I did. If not for prohibition, we'd be drinking champagne."

"Surely, Mary coming to Sinclair isn't that high of a celebration."

"No, but asking you to marry me is. Margaret Sinclair, will you marry me?"

Words I had spoken years ago haunt me. When did my mouth open? I snap it shut, blink rapidly several times, and find myself stuttering. "You... you... you want to court me? But, you don't know anything about me."

"But I do. I've gotten to know you through your father and grandfather. And, the moment I saw you weeks ago, I fell in love. Instantly. And, madly."

I'm stunned hearing him say this. I never had the impression he was in love with me—attracted yes, but love? He's never tried to kiss me. But then, what do I know about men and being in love? Other than what I've read in some novels and listening to the girls talk, I know next to nothing about love. I know what I felt for Johnny years ago was love, not like I love Grandfather and Father, but I was only six at the time. Puppy love, they call it. Adoration.

Admittedly, I am attracted. Is this what I'm feeling—love?

"I've been coming to see you every night, hoping to spark your interest." He pauses, searching my face for a reaction. Hopefully, a favorable one.

Slowly, I smile. "I'm interested." Actually, I'm flattered. Unlike Mary, I'm not one to express my excitement outwardly. And then, I realize— "Father! I can't just say yes without—"

"I have his blessing. Your grandfather's too."

"You sought their approval before asking me?"

"I didn't want you to be disappointed should they say no."

Obviously, this is a man who makes plans. I like it. I must admit, I enjoy being surprised, too.

"I've been courting you for weeks. Marry me."

Now, that I look back at these past few weeks, I can see that he has indeed been courting me. How could I have been so unaware?

By the time we return to the school, we've set a date for a mid-September wedding, and I've received my first kiss. One he gave me when we stepped outside of the restaurant.

It was good, I think, but since I have nothing to compare it to, how can it not be good?

I want to wait a year, but he convinced me that waiting that long would be unbearable. He wants us to get married sooner than that. In fact, he prefers an August wedding, but I insisted August is too soon. We settled on November close to Thanksgiving, a favorite holiday of mine.

As we talk and make plans for our future, I realize he's been considerate of my interests all along. How could I have been so blind?

Chapter 21*

Margaret

Two weeks later, I'm traveling home by ship as an engaged woman with a ring on my finger and a trousseau fit for a queen.

Before we left Detroit, Mary helped me shop and now travels with me as my companion, though I wish we weren't mistaken for each other anymore. She still finds it amusing.

As usual, I ignore it and am delighted to have her company through summer.

Frank is happy about it, too, saying I'll feel less lonely when he's not around. Apparently, he's got a lot of business to catch up on, telling me he'll be away on business more than he'd like.

She's going to teach me how to manage a household, a skill I desperately need and one where she's had lots of experience. In exchange, she gets a brief holiday before returning home and putting those skills to work, helping her mother.

She joins me at the steamer's rail. We're still a mile from Sinclair on Drummond Island, but I can point out its docks and Harbor House Island, a small island compared to the many other nearby islands, all much larger and situated between the two biggest: Drummond Island and St. Joseph Island.

So many more boats on Lake Huron than I remember from my childhood. Long barges traveling from Lake Superior and Lake Michigan, steaming their way to Detroit or eastern harbors. Lots of smaller boats, too. And, sail boats—the prettiest of all the boats.

From here, we can make out the Canadian shoreline. One

boat appears to be coming from Canada, heading for Michigan.

Seated passengers on rows of benches talk about the boat.

"Do you think any of them are involved with bootlegging?"

"From Canada?"

"Why not?"

"Mounties are probably patrolling."

Their voices fade away when I notice a man at the rail further down. I thought I'd seen everyone who was on board, given that the steamer was relatively small and acted like a ferry with only a few staterooms, one of which Mary and I shared last night. Given that our journey from Detroit to Drummond Island as it hugs Michigan's coastline was a little over 24 hours, most passengers slept sitting up on the benches—if they slept at all.

Must be that this stranger was in a stateroom the entire time. He's taller than most and wears a large-brimmed hat, one I once saw an Aussie wear. Other than his height and the hat, his clothing is typical. His stance, however, is atypical. His feet are spread apart and rooted to the deck as he surveys his surroundings. Like Frank and many men currently in fashion, he has a slight beard and mustache.

That's when he notices me watching. He tips his hat and bends his head slightly. His hair is as dark as his facial hair.

Even from this distance, the air sizzles with electricity. I shiver, and goosebumps pop out on my arms.

Who is he?

Mary tugs at my arm and points.

"Is that Harbor House Island? It's so small."

We're almost at the turning point where if we turn left, we'd be approaching Sinclair's multi-dock harbor, but if we were to turn right, we'd be heading toward Harbor House Island's two docks—one in front of the house and a shorter in front of the boathouse.

"Yes. It's a small island, a quarter mile long and half that across."

"Lots of trees."

"Only on the north and south shores. Grandfather cleared the land on the west and east, basically in front of the front and back doors. There's not a lot of land in the front, but more in the back. Mostly rocks on the Canadian side. Though even those areas look a bit overgrown now."

"The house is enormous. It looks like a medieval castle," she says.

I grin. "Probably why I liked it so much when I was younger."

The boat turns toward Sinclair's shores. Frank is there to greet us.

Minutes later, we dock, and the gangplank is positioned for disembarking.

Once we're ashore, Frank gives me a tight hug and a quick kiss, then hugs Mary. And then, he takes off his hat and reaches past me, shaking hands with someone.

I turn my head, shocked to see it's the stranger with the Aussie hat. The air around me crackles with electricity. The man's eyes—brown like Frank's—widen slightly. I glance at Mary and Frank. Am I imagining this charged atmosphere?

"Margaret," Frank says, "Meet the man who's going to help you restore Harbor House—Sawyer Van Houten."

Sawyer tips his hat.

I put out my hand. "How do you do?"

He takes it and squeezes slightly. A shock of energy catches me off guard. Quickly, I look down, remove my hand, then fumble with my handbag. I don't dare look at him again. I feel out of control. How in the world can these two men—Frank and

Sawyer—make me so aware of their energy like this? Because I have so little experience with men?

Frank says, "Your grandfather is expecting us for dinner."

"Let me help with the luggage," Sawyer says.

Mary and I head for the house. I'm grateful for the walk, putting some distance between the two men, even welcoming Mary's chatter. Thankfully, she's not asking any questions that I need to answer. Just gushing about everything she's seeing.

Quickly, we're at the house. It sits across the street from the docks and halfway up the hill, about half a block's distance. Sitting on the porch is always fun. Peaceful too, while watching the boats and dock activity.

Once Mary and I enter the house, I show her where our rooms are, so she can direct where the luggage should be delivered. Grandfather isn't in the house, so I go down to the kitchen to offer my help. With just one cook, she'll need more help. Even though I'm sure the cook has everything in hand, having a few more guests tonight could be a burden. It's not like I can cook, but I can cut, stir, and follow orders.

Minutes later, as I enter the dining room with the bread and butter, Grandfather calls out to me from his office. I set the dishes down and go to him. He's home.

As I enter the hall, Sawyer comes out of his office, nods, and walks away. I step into Grandfather's office.

"Shut the door," he says.

I do and then go around his enormous desk to give him a proper hug. He stands and we hug. It feels like he's hugging me tighter than when I last saw him, which wasn't that long ago.

"Welcome home. Congratulations on your engagement."

"Frank told you."

"He did. I approve."

"He said he wouldn't have proposed if you didn't. When

did he ask for your permission?"

"On the trip down to your coming out ball."

"That's a surprise. The first time I'd ever seen him was at the ball."

"He says he'd seen you on an earlier trip and fell in love with you at that first sighting. Think this old man has to have company to travel?"

I laughed. "No. And, you're not that old!"

"But, I am." He hands me some papers.

Last Will and Testament I read. I stare at Grandfather. "Why are you showing me this? Why now?" I hand them back.

"You aren't going to read it?"

"No."

"I don't want you to be surprised. I'm leaving you everything."

"What? Wait? No! What about Father? Doesn't he deserve—"

"No, he doesn't."

He sounds angry, defensive, and I detect a bit of sadness in his voice, too.

I gaze at this old man I love dearly and who, in just a few weeks since I've seen him, is looking frailer. What isn't he telling me?

"Are you sick?" I ask.

He laughs. "If it were only that simple. I know this is putting a lot on you, but trust me. I'm doing this with your best interest in mind. And, for the business."

A knock on the door, and the cook opens it. "Dinner's ready."

Grandfather nods.

He gets up, takes my hand, and pulls my hand and arm through his as he escorts me out of the room and into the dining room. Just before going through the arched doorway, he says, "We'll talk about it tomorrow, after you come back from giving Sawyer a tour of Harbor House and the island.

I open my mouth to object, but Frank is there and Grandfather hands me off to him. Frank seats me at the table so that I'm between Grandfather and him. Mary is across from me, between Grandfather and Sawyer.

Plans are made for Sawyer and me to visit Harbor House tomorrow. Mary asks if she can tag along, but Frank states he needs her help with his shopping. "It's a surprise," he says to me.

Grandfather states Sawyer will stay here while he's working on the house, but Sawyer counters.

"I'll be staying on the island once I get started. It's easier that way." He glances at Frank, who nods ever so slightly.

I look down at my napkin quickly to hide my expression. What was that nod about? Looking around the table, Mary is chatting with Sawyer and Frank with Grandfather. No one else saw it. I listen to the conversations, then suddenly feel extraordinarily tired and worried, too. Something isn't right, and I have no clue how to find out. All I can do is listen and observe.

Chapter 22*

Margaret

As it turns out, it's Mary and me who go to the island the next day. Grandfather sent Sawyer on a different errand out of town, and Frank postponed his and Mary's shopping trip because of an emergency client meeting, so he's left town, as well.

As Mary and I row the quarter mile toward the Island, I answer her questions about how Grandfather closed the house after Grandmother's death, and how my mother deserted my father and me shortly after my birth, with Grandfather raising me. I'm sure I told her all this when we were young. She probably forgot.

Once we land and tie up the boat, she loops her hand around my elbow, where I automatically crook my arm so we're walking arm-in-arm like we used to in school when sharing secrets and walking to our next class. "So, show me the house."

I do, and that's when I determine beyond any doubt that I want to live there. I don't mind its isolation.

We climb the front steps carefully, as a few of the steps need repair.

A large bell, twice my height, hangs from a wrought-iron hanger that juts out from the house just off the porch landing but easily within reach. Its bottom rim is level with my shoulders, and I can look up into it if I bend slightly and lean out beyond the landing a little. The bell looks old, like it came from a sunken ship. A frayed and weathered rope hangs from the clapper and is easy to access if I want to ring it.

Grandfather said he had installed it for Grandmother's sake when building the house. She was to ring it if she was ever in danger or needed help right away. He said she only rang it once—the day she died. It's been silent ever since.

I pull on the doorknob, and the door creaks and sticks a bit while opening.

Inside, there are cobwebs everywhere and lots of dust.

The house is immense, with a dozen bedrooms and a dining room that can easily seat thirty people, with fireplaces that we can stand in.

The old kitchen, a few steps lower than the rest of the house and at the back of the house, is a massive room and includes a small pantry. Grandfather had installed a pump for running water, which made it modern for its day. The kitchen will have to be remodeled right away.

Opposite the steps and door we just came through is another door. Opening it, there are a few steps down again and a longish hallway with one door at the end and another midway down the hall. An unlit lantern hangs on a wall, and the floor is earthen but packed down. My gut instinct tells me from previous occupants, occurring during the building of the home. It would make sense that the kitchen was built first, along with the house's foundation, so that the workers could be fed as they worked, allowing them to stay on the island as needed.

I go to the door midway down the hall and try to open it. "It feels locked. I wonder why. No other room in the house is locked."

Mary leans over and looks through the keyhole. "I don't see anything. What could be in there?"

She stands, and I look through the keyhole. Total darkness. I stand and look at the lock in puzzlement.

As I try the knob once more, Mary pulls me away. "What's

this other door?"

She opens it and we're outside in a small bit of yard encircled with trees and shrubs.

My face lights up. The view is spectacular. I imagine chairs out here.

"I know you well enough to know when inspiration has hit," she says.

She does. "I want to live here full time and turn the island and part of the home into a summer vacation retreat for friends and who want to get away from the city. Wouldn't it be marvelous seeing them again? Having them visit in the summer?"

Mary looks around.

I know what she's seeing. She's seeing reality, while I'm seeing possibilities. She sees cobwebs, dark, closed-up rooms that haven't seen daylight in twenty years. I see guests mingling in bright, sunny rooms.

"I think you're crazy to want to do this."

A wolf howls from a neighboring island.

"And, he just agreed with me," she adds.

I probably am crazy, but it's a wonderful idea knowing I own this. I'm still amazed by it all.

A dozen steps away from the house, there's shrubbery and a few skinny trees. She points to an opening in the brush. A deer trail? I don't see any tracks, but obviously it's an animal path of some kind—wide and well-trodden.

If Grandfather had this cleared out at one time, nature has taken over. I want it cleared out again so anyone sitting here in the yard can have a view of the lake.

"Where does this go?" she asks.

"To the lake. To the Canadian beachside of the island." Minutes later, we find a rocky beach with a few spots of sand. I look across Lake Huron and can just make out the Canadian coastline.

"Look!" She takes a few steps onto the beach and plucks a piece of bright green sea glass from the sand. "I wonder if there's more." We search and find some more pieces. White, pink, more green, and a blue one.

I stumble. Next to my foot is a half-buried, dark brown bottle. Empty with no label. Apparently, it had washed up on shore. Where had it come from? Had it been in the water longer, would it have become sea glass? I pick it up to take home.

Chapter 23

Hunter

Present Day

The three of us stand in the front parlor of Harbor House, the main room to the left of the entry hall.

The house is in better condition than I had imagined. But, it still needs work. I'm not about to reveal my true feelings to Mars and Amanda who look as if they've just stepped inside a house of horror. Only because it's dark, the room looks old and huge and feels spooky.

A smattering of dried brown leaves has been blown against the walls, circling the room. I half expect to find broken windows, but Drew told me that several severely cracked windows and a broken one had been repaired recently, the result of a brutal storm. I wonder why the room wasn't swept during the repair, though. With the curtains closed, the room is gloomy. Light spills into the room as I open them and the gloom disappears.

Soot from the fireplace appears as if it had climbed out of the chimney and crept across the mantel and up the wallpaper. There's a faint outline of a picture that once hung on the wall above the fireplace.

"This isn't creepy," Amanda says, her voice dripping with sarcasm.

"Kind of disgusting," Mars adds.

I open a window to let fresh air in. The house had been closed for too long. A screech sounds.

Is that an owl? Like the image on the box? Surprisingly, there are no screens. Will that be true of the entire house? I suspect it may be. Don't they have mosquitoes up here? Something I'll have to fix if I'm to stay.

Behind us, a bell rings. Just one ring. Not even a full ring. More like a timid ding. I go to the front door and step out onto the stoop. The other two follow me.

On our way inside, I didn't notice the huge bell hanging just beyond the right edge of the stoop, and high enough to be out of sight because of the tree in front of it.

The rope to ring it hangs nearly to the ground and is within reach when standing at the edge of the stoop.

Mounted on wrought iron connected to the house, the bell is old but not green with age. I wonder about its metal composition. I'd bet I could stand within the bell easily. It's that large.

Amanda reaches for the rope.

I stop her, grabbing her arm. "Don't."

"Why not?"

"I think it's used as a warning device."

"How do you know that?" Mars asks.

"I read it in the notes Drew gave me. It's the bell that alerts those on the big island that something is wrong." They look at me as if I've grown a second head suddenly.

They haven't read the papers that Drew gave me. Papers that included the police report written up in 1924. It was hearing the bell that brought others from Drummond Island to Harbor House Island, where they had discovered the horror of Margaret's murder. Even in the report, it says the bell had only been used three times. Once, when George Sinclair's wife died—of natural causes and was alone on the island at the time, other than one servant. When Margaret Sinclair was giving birth, alerting her husband. A servant had rung it that time, too. And then, the third time, alerting others of the imminent danger, but no one knew who had rung it.

But, if the bell was rung only in times of danger, why had it just dinged? More like a *tink.* Just enough to get our attention. Was it meant to get my attention?

Am I in danger?

I look around the yard and out at the dock. There's no one else here on the island. Just us three.

"The wind must have done it," Mars says.

"But there isn't any wind," Amanda counters.

She's right. The treetops are still with no grasses moving, including the shrubbery. Looking out at Lake Huron, the water is smooth, like glass. No waves. Inspecting the bell, I realize that as thick as the rope is, it would take a strong gale-force wind to move it. Even then, it would have to be a swirling wind to fully ring the bell.

"That's odd," Mars says. "There's always wind on Michigan's waterfronts."

Immediately, a powerful gust of wind blows across the stoop, lifting my hair. The bell's rope remains stationary. That's when I notice just past the stoop, the rope is snagged in a bracket meant to keep the rope from swaying in any breeze. So much for a gale-force wind.

If the rope is secured, how could it have tinked just now?

Mars squats and picks up a toothpick, stuffing it in his pocket. Quietly, I sigh. I hope he won't litter this property with his toothpicks, like he does in Detroit.

But wait, he didn't have a toothpick in his mouth when we arrived or have his hands in his pockets, so where did it come from? I don't remember seeing it on the ground before, and I always notice them when Mars is around, seeing him toss them.

He didn't toss this one. He picked it up instead.

He and Amanda go back inside.

I stand staring at the bell and then at Sinclair and its docks.

A warm breeze with the scent of lilacs overwhelms me. Even though a breeze swirls around me, nothing else moves. Not the plants, the trees, or even the few colored leaves on the ground heralding fall.

So where did the lilac scent come from?

Chapter 24

Hunter

As we first walked up to the house, I took note of the tiled roof. The tiles will probably last through my lifetime. Now, having looked around inside and outside, it appears no expense was spared when building this place.

Looking around the yard, I see a wide stand of old lilac bushes that are twice as tall as the stone shed that stands at the edge of the bushes furthest away from me. Because it's early fall, there are no blossoming flowers anywhere. Colored leaves on the trees heavily hint at the colder weather that will arrive soon.

Are these the lilac bushes that Margaret's grandmother planted, which would make them over 100 years old? Appears that way to me.

I wonder what's stored in the shed. Tools perhaps? I'll have to search it later.

I walk around the yard a bit, checking out the plants.

When I finally go inside, I find Mars and Amanda in the kitchen, which is the most livable room in the house right now. It's a few steps down from the rest of the house, built as if it were an addition. To the left is the full kitchen, U-shaped, with a huge wooden island in the center. I want to save this butcher block and have it incorporated into a larger island, one with storage and seating to replace the small table with four chairs next to the current island. To my right are cabinets and a broom closet. A door by the sink leads to a small pantry.

Across the room, in line with the door we just came

through, is another door. Mars has his hand on the doorknob.

He opens it. A few more stairs. He steps down, looking on either side. "There's no light switch."

Seeing a plate of switches above the countertop near the door, I flip a switch. One lone bare bulb on the ceiling creates a dim light. Another door is at the end of the hall.

Mars goes and opens it. A breeze flows past us, as Amanda and I step down, entering the hallway. It's the back entrance to the house, and the breeze is coming from Lake Huron from the Canadian side, wafting through the kitchen and into the rest of the house.

Halfway through the hall, a stack of wood lines the middle portion of one wall. No wonder it smells so musty down here. Plus, the floor is dirt. Packed hard.

The walls are dark and look like paneling. The darkest woodgrain paneling ever. I reach out to touch it. Instantly, my hand feels cold, and then the cold moves past me. "Did you guys feel that?"

They are returning to the kitchen and have their backs to me. They pause on the stairsteps and look back at me.

"Feel what?" Amanda asks.

"A cold spot."

She laughs. "You're imagining things."

"No, she isn't," Mars counters. "It's an old house. People were murdered here, died here."

"Only one I know of," I inject.

He finishes with, "There could be cold spots."

Another wave of cold washes over me and what feels like a scratch on the back of my neck. It's as if someone just passed through me. I shiver, no doubt my face registering surprise. I raise my hand to the back of my neck but can't feel anything.

Amanda laughs again. "Okay, okay. Sure, why wouldn't

there be ghosts here? I get it."

That she is still chuckling is telling. It's her nervous laugh, which makes little sense. She believes in ghosts. We've certainly talked about it often enough, especially after watching a movie that features them.

Could she actually be fearful of ghosts when it comes to experiencing or facing them? That she doesn't want to encounter anything like that here, even remotely? That it's all just bravado in the world of literature and movies, but in real life, she's truly frightened?

So, why aren't I afraid like her? I've never experienced anything like this either. Am I open to these thoughts because of Margaret and this house?

I step over to the outside door, shut it, and lock it, then follow them up the few stairs. Grabbing the doorknob, I start closing the door, but take one last look into the hall to make sure I'm not missing anything.

What do I expect to see? An orb? A misty form?

I switch off the tunnel hall light. It doesn't feel like a hallway anymore. Now it's an endless dark tunnel. Shutting the door soundly, I pull on the knob, just to make sure the door is latched properly. I don't want it creaking open on its own.

For any reason.

I wonder if I should change the locks.

Once we've inspected the house thoroughly, we meet in the front parlor and sit on the sheet-draped couches.

I have no idea what kind of furniture we'll find under all the sheets, but I'm glad that the people who controlled the trust didn't sell all of Sawyer and Margaret's furniture. Drew had mentioned that some of it was the original post-Civil War furniture that George Sinclair and his bride had purchased.

"Now that you've both seen it all, what do you think?" I ask.

"I don't want to influence you," Mars says. "Shouldn't we know what you're thinking first?"

Amanda nods. "What do you want to do?"

I'm nervous about telling them because I don't want them to think I'm going crazy, but we all do crazy things at thirty, right?

I've been in a dead-end job even though I loved it. If I went back, I'd never make much more than I had been making, though of course, over time, there'd be cost-of-living raises. With that salary, it would take forever to save enough money for a B&B. Inheriting this house solves that problem. It all but screams, *Turn me into a B&B!*

How can I say no?

"I want to move here for good and turn this place into my home and a bed and breakfast. I did the research before we came up here. The potential for it to succeed is strong." I honey up to Mars with, "And, with the right promotional director who knows graphic designs—"

"Sure, I'd be happy to help you, providing I get to stay—*free!*—anytime I come visit."

"Deal!" I stick out my hand. He shakes it.

"But, how can you possibly make it work?" Amanda asks. "You don't have a job."

"Well, Mom and Dad's house is completely paid for. They'd paid it off long ago, so anything I get from the insurance company and the sale of the house—even though it'll be a fire sale—with some of their furniture, that'll give me income I can live on for a couple of years."

I pull out the list that's in my pocket and hand it to them. Their heads come together as they share the list between them so they can both read it at the same time.

Mars whistles.

"Wow, I'm impressed," Amanda says. "You really thought this through."

"Including what will happen should this place fail to earn an income," I say. "I can use my inheritance money from the Sinclair trust to upgrade this place, but I'll have to be careful and not overspend beyond it. It'll take careful planning and going step-by-step to get this place in shape, and it needs to be done quickly."

"Doing a lot of the work yourself?" Mars asks.

"As much as I possibly can, though, I know I'll have to hire some out, too."

"So, where does that leave Mars and me? And, for how long?" Amanda asks.

"Well, you two were willing to spend two weeks up here. Would you be willing to do some work during these next two weeks?"

They look at each other, then back and me, both grinning and reaching out an arm with their hands in front of me, their two hands stacked. Immediately, I placed my hand on top of theirs.

Together we say, "All for one, and one for all."

Yeah, corny, I know, but it works for us and makes us laugh, just as we are doing now.

"Guess it's a good thing we each drove up here separately, given that you're staying," Mars says.

Amanda puffs out her lower lip, pretending to pout. "I don't want to go back to work! I want to stay here and adventure with you!"

"I doubt it's going to be much of an adventure, what with all the cleaning that needs to be done." My gaze moves around the room. I'm hoping for minimal damage given how the trust cared for the house. I want to install a few bathrooms, remodel the kitchen, and modernize the electrical, plumbing, and heating systems to today's standards. Most of that will be hired.

I'll have to see if there are any zoning restrictions, too.

We talk for the next hour and determine how we'll clean the place up first.

Sweep it. Remove the sheets covering the furniture. Then, they'll help me inventory each room and its furniture and provide ideas for remodeling or sprucing up.

We talk about the supplies we brought: bedding and sleeping bags—just in case—food, a vacuum, cleaning supplies, and what we still need from the big island as we decide we'll stay here rather than at a motel on Drummond.

We'll have to go shopping for more food, and I want to see about getting a washer and dryer installed. I don't feel like rowing or boating my laundry across the lake to the laundromat every week.

While having a rowboat is nice, the motorized bigger boat—both mine—that we had crossed with is a more efficient mode of travel. I was told that the rowboat is in the boathouse.

When we had docked, I saw a second, shorter dock next to the boathouse. I wonder if, in the short distance between the two islands, the water freezes during winter and if the boats get stored. If the water freezes, does that mean we hike across the lake? What about a snowmobile? I'll have to look in the boathouse. All things to be discovered later.

Thankfully, the electricity hasn't ever been turned off, so the stove and refrigerator—an old DOMELERE—are working, though they weren't plugged in when we arrived. Mars volunteers to go to the big island for groceries. The refrigerator isn't much more than a box with some coils, but until we can get a new refrigerator installed, it'll do. Mars is excited to see that it has a couple of ice cube trays, which he fills immediately. Knowing him, he'll probably pick up a bottle of whisky. For celebration purposes, as he always says.

I tell Mars to get a cooler just in case. With some ice. Given the icebox's age, I'm reluctant to trust it one hundred percent.

While Mars is gone, Amanda and I finish inventorying the rooms. She has several good ideas but doesn't have quite the vision I have. She sees the place as fixed up and modern. I want to keep its historic charm. At least in these front sitting rooms, dining room, den, and maybe a few of the bedrooms upstairs.

As usual, I let her talk and express her ideas, writing them down, but on a separate sheet of paper that I can dispose of later. She likes to think her ideas are wonderful, and they are. For her.

She never seems to fully understand how different we are, even though we have several similarities.

The day disappears once we discover that cleaning up a room together goes faster than each of us doing rooms separately. We talk, laugh, and reminisce about the past. Plus, once Mars returns, they help with moving furniture as we decide what to keep in each room and what to take out. For now, we move what we won't be using into the wide hall if downstairs, and into one of the spare bedrooms if upstairs. I may want to recycle some of it later. To store it, there has to be an attic, but we haven't found it yet.

As we work together, it feels like old times.

We've done a lot today, and there's just as much to do tomorrow, so we stop when our stomachs begin growling.

After fixing our sandwiches in the kitchen, we bring our food into the dining room and sit at one end of the table. Amanda sits at the head, with Mars and me on either side.

"Can't you just see the table filled with summer guests," I coo. I'm still enthralled with the historic features of the house. After much discussion with Mars, we decide I need to investigate hiring a restoration expert, especially if I'm interested in preserving any of the wallpaper. Looking at this room's wallpaper, I can't determine its age. I suspect that only the absolute best wallpaper had been purchased and installed. Much like everything else in the house. I wonder if the wallpaper is original to when the house was built. I hope it is. I'm hoping I can wash it, especially above any fireplace.

The house has been well taken care of, despite all the leaves that had blown into the front parlor. Fortunately, the leaves didn't do any damage.

After 100 years of being sealed up tight, there is no water damage anywhere, the doors and windows open and shut properly despite any summer humidity as an island house. Even more amazing is the lack of spiderwebs. Untypical of a deserted property.

It's almost as if someone has lovingly been taking care of it all these years. Keeping it swept, casting out any spiders. There aren't even any mouse droppings anywhere either. Is that because of the stone foundation instead of wood? I have no idea. More questions to ask the trust holders who cared for the business and properties.

As we eat, we talk about our plans for tomorrow. We're going to the big island, me to the library, Mars to pick up home repair supplies, and Amanda...she can't decide what she wants to do. She talks about going to the larger community on the other side of Drummond Island opposite Sinclair. But, she doesn't say why either. In the end, she mumbles something about tagging along with Mars.

It isn't late by the time we finish and have dinner cleaned up, but it's been a long day. The two of them want to walk the shoreline on the Canadian side. I retire to my room instead.

Daisy follows me up the stairs as I carry her second bed with me. For now, the first one sits in the dining room, but I'm not sure where its ultimate home will be. I'll have to find out where she most favors sleeping downstairs and will place a bed there. This bed, though, will be close to my bed.

I've chosen what I believe was Margaret's room—the turret room. The bed is an ornate four-poster bed. Earlier, I put clean sheets on it, not wanting to use my sleeping bag. Surprisingly, all the bedrooms' bedspreads and comforters aren't dusty. Did whoever was cleaning the house regularly also tend to the comforters and other bedding?

By the time I change into PJs, Daisy is already curled in her bed and asleep. I'm tired but not ready to close my eyes yet. Next to the bed is a nightstand with several drawers. There's nothing of interest until I open the bottom drawer. Some old-fashioned cloth handkerchiefs, the kind women would have used at the turn of the last century. But then, I notice that the space is half that of the drawer's true depth. I pull out the handkerchiefs and see a tiny slit at the front of the drawer on its floor. It almost looks like a scratch. I reach for my purse and find my metal nail file. Poking the file's point into the slit, I'm able to lift the floor up and out of the drawer.

Has this been a hidden piece of history all this time?

Inside is a handmade box, a duplicate of the box with the owl carving. This one has a flowering branch of some kind.

I try the lid. It's locked.

Looking at the keyhole, it looks just like the first box. Is it possible that the key inside that first box is the key to this one?

Reaching into my purse again, I dig out the key.

With it in hand, I pick up the box and sit cross-legged on the double bed, insert the key, and open the box.

The scent of lilacs is immediate. Not overwhelmingly strong but just enough that I recognize it. I close the box and re-examine the carving. Yup, now I can see it. Lilacs.

If Margaret's grandmother had planted the lilacs, was this Margaret's grandmother's box?

I open the box again. A leather-bound book as long and wide as the box, with a strap around its width, rests neatly within. If not for the middle strap, I would have missed it because the cover's leather is the same color as the box's interior.

I pull the book out, setting the box aside. Undoing the strap, I open the cover. Beautiful cursive writing fills the pages. No identification as to whose book it is, though. Flipping through the pages clearly identifies it as a journal or a diary of some sort.

The first entry has no date either.

I'd been fascinated with Harbor House from the time I first saw it as a youngster standing on Sinclair's shores. I'd go stand on the highest rocks so I could get a full glimpse of the house's towering turret. Even then, I knew that one day I'd have a bedroom in that turret.

This diary has to be Margaret's. Her grandmother was already married to George when the house was built. Margaret was born in Sinclair and lived there before she was sent to a boarding school when she was six. I can easily picture her standing on Sinclair's rocks, looking at this bedroom, which is in the only turret, giving it multiple window views of Lake Huron both in the north and in the south, plus a view of Sinclair's docks and shoreline.

I love that I've now inherited this bedroom. It's my favorite room in the house. I feel strongly connected to these two amazing ladies.

The room is big enough that I could set up a desk and write and manage the business, or I could put a desk in what used to be the nursery. A small room off this one. Earlier we moved the large cradle bassinet into another bedroom. Because of the size of this room, I can easily put a desk in front of the fireplace or under a window. Yes. That way, I can use the smaller room as both a closet and a storage center for my personal belongings. If the rest of the house is going to be a B&B, I don't want my stuff scattered around the house.

The more I think about it, the better I like this idea. Thumbing through the diary's pages as I'm thinking, I came to the last entry.

For the last few days, I've had a sense of foreboding, but I can't attach the feeling to anything going on here in the house, the island, or even in Sinclair.

And yet...

It feels like something evil is coming this way.

This had to have been Margaret's box. But, if this was her box, whose box was the first one with the owl carving? Had she known about it? She had to have. Drew said the first box was among Margaret's possessions.

This second box had been hidden. No one other than Margaret and now me has ever seen this journal.

Could this box have been her grandmother's, which she then started using? Would that have made the owl-carved box her grandfather's?

I want to believe that Margaret loved lilacs as much as her grandmother because the room is the epitome of lilacs. The wallpaper in here is a faint purple and cream with sprigs of lilacs, and now this box. Even the sheer curtains at the windows are light purple. Or, did Margaret just keep it that way for the love of her grandmother whom she never knew?

Can the curtains in this house really be a hundred years old, or have they been duplicated and replaced at one time or another?

I frown, looking at the curtains. Now, that I think about it, those curtains should have been dusty, but they aren't. In fact, this entire room appears to have been thoroughly cleaned recently. Has it been? Has the entire house been cleaned periodically despite it sitting empty for so long?

I made a mental note to stop at the lawyer's office tomorrow and ask some questions before going to the library.

Even though the office is where I picked up the keys to the house and the boat when I first arrived in Sinclair, I had met only the assistant who sat at the front desk. The people I needed to meet were occupied in meetings. Hopefully, I'll get lucky tomorrow and can meet with one of the Trust's officers without having an appointment.

I get up and turn off the lights except for the one by my bedside. At the windows, I close them because it's raining now, with the rain coming inside.

Pulling down the covers, I crawl between the sheets and get settled. I pick up the journal and start reading again, going back to the beginning and where I had left off. Margaret was writing about how she had met Johnny and how he became her hero. The boy she had asked to marry her when she was six and he was eleven.

*****

I wake with a start.

Sitting up, I look around.

BANG!

I jump.

I fell asleep while reading. The bedside lamp is still on.

The bang sounds again, and then again, but not as loud.

Something is bumping against the house just outside my window.

I curl back the covers and pad over to the window.

A shutter is loose.

I open the window and reach out, grabbing the shutter as

the wind flutters it away from the house and toward me. At least the rain has stopped. I'm able to latch it from here, essentially shuttering this side of the window. With the shutter blocking the window, I leave the window itself open so I can hear nature's night noises.

I'll have to wait until tomorrow to see how to secure it properly to the house. A task I don't want to undertake in the dark.

One more thing to add to my to-do list, I think as I stare out toward the lake and Sinclair. It's so dark, I can't see anything beyond my dock, except for a few streetlights near Sinclair's docks.

Daisy growls. I turn, frowning. What is she upset about?

She's staring at the bedroom's closed door.

I listen.

I hear nothing.

She trots over to the door and sniffs. She growls softly again, snorts, turns around, returns, and sits next to where I stand. She looks up at me as if to say, *I've got you.*

And then, I hear what sounds like voices.

I go to my bedside table and turn off the light. The room plunges into darkness.

Voices come from what sounds like outside. But how can that be?

I step over to the window, move the flimsy curtain aside, open the non-shuttered window, raising the window up fully so I can stick my head out.

Laughter.

Faint, not close by.

Nothing moves on this island or its dock, which I can see from here. I look beyond my shoreline and across the short distance to the big island. With the rain stopped, I can see across the lake. It's easy to see two figures move on the dock, and then I hear splashes, screams, and more laughter.

A pair of lovers, maybe. Swimming in the dark. Probably nude and drinking, too. The water must be cold.

It's amazing how their voices travel across the water. I'll have to remember that. I don't want my conversations overheard like that.

Out of the corner of my eye, I see movement. Turning my head slightly, I'm looking at the lilacs. If I didn't know better, I could swear someone was moving within them. I blink, refocusing.

Shadows. Nothing but shadows I'm not familiar with.

An owl hoots.

Goosebumps crawl up and down my arms.

Daisy growls again. Only this time, she's facing the other side of the room that is so dark I can barely make out the chair in front of the fireplace. I can't see into the corners at all. She stands on four legs, braced as if ready to charge. Her growl threatening.

The owl hoots again. Its call is clear and close by. I wonder if it's sitting on a nearby branch watching me.

Daisy rubs up against my leg. I look down. Her tongue hangs out as she pants a little. The fearsome, protective creature I just saw is gone. I reach down and scratch the top of her head. She retreats to her bed, but I notice she rests her chin on the edge of her bed while looking toward that dark corner.

I close both windows as it starts raining again and go back to bed.

Chapter 25

Hunter

Birds chirping outside my window wake me up. I smile, listening.

Opening my eyes, billowing curtains drift to their hanging position with the collapse of a breeze. Then, they're billowing again.

Wait a minute!

I sit up, startled.

I went to bed after shutting the windows. Now, they're open. And, the half that should still be shuttered is completely free of the shutter.

Going to the window, I stick my head out. The shutter that was flapping last night is now against the house and fastened.

How can that be? I hadn't done it. Had someone come into the room while I was asleep?

And, where is Daisy? She's gone.

*****

Minutes later, dressed, and ready for a short boat ride across the lake and an excursion to the library and lawyer's office, I step into the hall to look for Daisy and nearly crash into Mars.

"Morning. You slept in late. I hope you don't mind that I let Daisy out. She was scratching at the door."

"What? You took Daisy? When have you ever favored her?"

"Long night?" he asked. "I tried waking you."

I paused. "Actually, yes. I'm sorry. Did you open my windows and fix the shutter, too?"

"I did. I hope you don't mind that I came in while you were sleeping."

"No...yes...no. Surprised, yes. But, considering how much I enjoyed waking up to the birds, no."

"I won't make it a habit."

"I'll be down in a minute," I say. Going back into my room, I chastise myself for not saying I am bothered he came into my room while I was asleep. While I appreciate his being kind to Daisy, at the same time, his behavior doesn't make sense. Why now? Letting Daisy out, I understand, but how did he know the shutter had come loose last night? First, he secretly got my DNA and created an account in my name, and now this?

What else could he have done?

Can I continue to trust him? Should I? I shiver, goosebumps crawling over my skin. Before arriving here, I never got goosebumps. I can count on one hand the number of times they occurred. But, since arriving here...?

Something strange is happening. Both in the house and within me. I shiver with goosebumps again at that thought.

What does it all mean?

I grab my purse and shut the door, leaving my room.

*****

I hear Mars and Amanda's laughter before I join them in the kitchen, where they're making breakfast.

Daisy, who is here with them, whines. Opening the back kitchen door, we go down the few steps and through the hall, where I open the outside door. I wait while she does her business, then shut the door, sliding the bolt, and locking it. Retracing our steps, I shut the kitchen hallway door, too.

The three of us are standing around the island, gobbling our food so we can get going.

Amanda pokes me.

She's staring at the hallway door.

It's opening.

Slowly.

On its own.

Then suddenly, it slams shut!

All three of us jump.

"What was that?" Mars asks.

Amanda yells. "That's crazy!"

I'm speechless. I just stare. Goosebumps crawl up and down my arms again. How is it unlocked?

I go to the door and open it.

I gasp.

The door at the other end of the hall is open. I had locked it, too. I know I did. How could it possibly be unlocked?

A wind blows through the hall, a breeze that lifts the edges of my hair off my shoulders. An icy breeze. The outside air isn't that cold. What's going on?

Mars, who stands behind me, laughs. "Oh, it's just the wind."

"I don't think I could stand knowing it's a ghost," Amanda adds.

"Can you go shut that door?" I ask Mars, indicating the outer door.

He moves around me and shuts it quickly and efficiently. Coming back into the kitchen, he crosses his arms, clapping his biceps. "Brr, that's one cold hallway."

I don't have the guts to ask if he just walked through a cold spot or if it was cold air coming in from outside. After last night and now this?

Something strange is going on. No question about it. But ghosts?

No, I've read too many novels.

It's an old house, yes, and deserted for a long time, yes. A house I'm not familiar with. No doubt the floors aren't level, the doors aren't level either, and the locks aren't latching securely.

The thing I can't shake is that I *know* I locked both doors. Solidly. And, then suddenly, they're both open.

I need to find someone who deals with ghosts, spirits, or whatever they call what is happening here.

Chapter 26

Hunter

Half an hour later, we dock our boat and agree to meet at a Sinclair restaurant for dinner before returning to the island.

My first stop is at the lawyer's office. I get lucky and talk with the lawyer who manages the trust. I need to sign final papers while I'm here, which makes everything now legally mine. I ask if they can still manage the business on my behalf as they've been doing, and he agrees.

When I ask questions about the house, he informs me that indeed, over the years, the house was maintained and cleaned regularly. In fact, a team is scheduled to come in to clean the following week. Do I still want them to come?

I almost say no, but then decide, why not? They have a routine and no doubt the supplies we found once we began cleaning must belong to them. I tell him we used some of the supplies.

"Not a problem," he says.

"Is it possible to have someone check the fireplaces?" I ask. Even though we probably wouldn't use them during our stay, I'm already thinking ahead to the possibility if I do stay.

"Most certainly, we can do that. Twice a year, we checked the deterrents we had installed to keep birds out of the chimneys, making sure they were still in place and doing their job. Since no one was burning any fires, once we had cleaned them all, we inspected them periodically rather than every year, but we can certainly check them now, to insure their safe to use."

I'm about to ask him about finding a ghost hunter, but out of nowhere, a voice only I can hear tells me not to. That this man in front of me isn't the right person to ask.

"Are you all right?" he asks.

"Ye...yeah, I'm fine." But I'm not. *What* was that? I've never heard a voice like that before. Apparently, he didn't hear it. Just me. Lucky me.

Minutes later, my business with the lawyer is done, and I make an appointment for two weeks. At that time, I'll either be selling the place or wanting to know more about the business because I'm staying.

My next stop is the library.

I find a few books about Drummond Island and Sinclair in general and about logging in Michigan but nothing about the families. Usually, when there is a local murder, someone will author a book about it. This murder was almost one hundred years ago. Would there still be interest even if only local interest?

"Excuse me." I'm at the front desk, having approached a woman with gray hair and a pencil holding her topknot at the top of her head. Large glasses frame big brown eyes. A librarian would know if any books had been written about this community. With any luck, she's a lifelong resident and knows the community's history well. "My name is Hunter Marshall—"

"Oh, you're Margaret's granddaughter—"

"Great granddaughter."

The librarian laughs. "Of course. I bet you're looking for information about the family."

"Yes." I can't help but grin. I stick out my hand. "I'm a librarian—well, was before I was let go a week ago."

She shakes my hand, her eyes sparkling. "I'm Lolly Pine."

"Lolly?"

"Pine," she adds. "And, yes, they did it. My parents. Naming me after a tree, but only with the first name. I married a Pine. My parents worked for the senior Sinclair when they were teenagers. Worked for the company their entire lives. I appeared late in their lives. At a time, when their peers were retiring."

Lolly leads me to the archive section, all the while talking about the Sinclair family. She sets me up with computer files and paper files, directing me to specific dates to search for. Instinctively, she knows I want to read and make copies of everything I can find.

"What about the bell?" I ask. "I've heard that it was used for emergencies and that the only time it rang was when anyone was in trouble."

"Yes. Margaret rang it when she went into labor, but no one knows who rang it the second time when she was murdered. She died upstairs in her bedroom."

"What about her husband? Was he a suspect?"

"There's no way Sawyer would have harmed a hair on Margaret's head. That man adored her and their baby. He would have given up his life to protect her."

"But, he was never found."

"No, that's the sad part. No one knows what happened to him. Vanished. Disappeared completely. My parents talked about him often. The entire Sinclair family was held in high esteem, well, except for Margaret's father, Edward. Tragic what happened to him because others preyed upon his weaknesses."

"You're talking about Frank Darnell, now, aren't you? As one of those who preyed?"

She nods. "He was such a stalwart citizen when he first arrived in Sinclair. Appeared to be anyhow. Became a backbone of the community, and then it was discovered he'd been using the Sinclair family from the beginning. Good riddance, I say."

"He was never found either?"

"No. Ironic how both men disappeared. A good man and an evil one. Two sides of the same coin."

"How so?"

"Because they both were in love with Margaret."

"Over the years, has anything new developed, anything strange?"

Lolly glances past me, scoping our surroundings. Is she checking to make sure no one can hear us? She leans in closer and speaks just above a whisper. "As a little girl, I used to see lights over on the island and once in a while from an upstairs window."

Goosebumps slide across my arms. "Which window?" I whisper back.

"From the turret second floor."

Margaret's room. The room I'm sleeping in. Hairs on the back of my neck tickle. "What kind of light?"

"Almost as someone—or something—was passing the window. A shadow but one of light."

"A lantern?"

"I don't know. The light was dim, shadowy, not bright, and it never flickered."

"What about more recently?"

"Some of the men who go out fishing early in the morning, and who are at the piers before daybreak, swear they can see someone walking around the outside of the house before disappearing into the shrubbery."

"And...?"

"Nothing else. You know how just before dawn and being on the shore can create misty shadows."

"No, I can't say that I'm familiar with that experience. Not yet, anyway."

"You'll experience it if the weather turns or you're here for any length of time. I just question what they're really seeing."

I ask, "Who was responsible for the lilac wallpaper in the bedroom? Do you know?"

"That'd be Margaret. Even though her grandmother had planted the lilac bushes out in the yard, it was Margaret who brought the icons into the house." Lolly's face lights up with excitement. "I think I've got a picture of Margaret standing in front of the lilacs. I'll be right back." She disappears into the office area. A minute later, she returns with a shoebox in her hands. "Let's go into a private room," she says, leading the way.

I follow her toward the back of the library and into a small room where she sets the box on the table and pulls out a chair. I pull out a chair next to hers.

Once we're both seated, she pushes up the lid, removing it, and casting it to the side. Inside are dozens of old photos. She scoops them out and places them on the table, pushing the box aside.

"We have dreams of one day getting all the files and pictures we've inherited, been given, and have found over the years through various local estate sales into the computer archives. But, with the downsizing of staff, we don't have a lot of spare time to get the job done."

"It's why I was let go," I tell her. "Maybe I can volunteer and help out." As soon as I say the words, I regret having said them. Who knows how long I'll be here? And, if I stay, can I afford to be just a volunteer? Would I need a job? I'll be running a B&B, but will it be profitable?

Lolly appears excited at the idea.

Before she can say anything, I counter with, "If I'm here long enough."

"Oh, you're not staying long?"

"I don't know." My gaze goes to the pictures.

She thumbs through a few of them and pulls one out of the

pile. "Here it is!" She hands it to me.

A young woman, who appears to be in the early stages of pregnancy, stands in front of some bushes that are twice as tall as she is.

"The lilac bushes?" I ask.

"Yes."

"They've grown quite a bit over the years."

"They're probably forty years old in this picture. Brought in as mature plants. Notice how they've spread and are thick even then."

"Thicker now," I say. "Can't even see through them to the other side. You've been to the island?"

"Not in recent years, but I did go over with one cleaning team one year. They needed extra help. Every few years, they'd do a huge spring cleaning. I took a few cuttings of the lilacs, but they didn't survive. Those lilacs must be huge by now and spread outward more than twice what's shown here."

"They have." I hand the picture back to her.

"Would you like a copy?"

"Yes, please, I would."

"Take a look through the rest of the photos and if you see any others of the family or the house you'd like to have, we can make copies of those, too." She starts to leave, but then turns back, putting the photo on the corner of the table. "Why don't I leave this here until you've had a chance to go through the others? That way we can make copies of everything all at one time."

"Okay."

"Just bring the box back to the desk when you're done." And then, she leaves me alone with the pictures.

Taking my time, I look at each photo carefully and flip it over, hoping for identification clues.

Have these photographs all come from the Sinclair estate, or do they include pictures from other estates? Given the number of pictures here, I have to believe it's the latter.

Suddenly, toward the end of the pile, the content changes. Up until now, most of the pictures were of Sinclair, with buildings being erected, various Fourth of July picnics throughout the years, and a few winter scenes of snow so high in town that tunnels went to the buildings' doors with only the second story visible. It was such a tiny village back then.

In these last couple dozen pictures, one man is featured and always with a different group of people. Fortunately, on the back of each picture, the people are identified. The featured man is the elder George Sinclair, the patriarch and owner of Sinclair Lumber, and there are two pictures of Margaret and Sawyer's wedding. At least, I assume so as Margaret stands between her grandfather and Sawyer while holding a bouquet, reminiscent of a bridal bouquet.

Then, a picture of the island house again with a policeman standing on the stoop, his hand on the bell's rope. A faint orb is in the doorway, so light in color that someone unfamiliar with orbs would have missed it. Glancing at the lilac bushes just at the picture's left edge. I notice there's a second orb.

I've seen orbs in photos Mars and Amanda took of me in the house and the backyard after Mom and Dad had died. There were always two orbs, often close together. I never knew what they were until a neighbor, when looking at the pictures, told me. At the time, I didn't know whether to believe her or not. However, that discussion sent me to research orbs. Even after my research, I still wasn't sure what to believe.

But now...?

Had Mom and Dad's spirits surrounded me all along, with me not knowing it?

Is it possible I'm seeing the orb spirits of family members who once lived here? If so, who? Sawyer and Margaret? George Sinclair and his wife? Someone else?

After going through the entire box of pictures, I have a small pile of about a dozen pictures I want copied. Including the ones with orbs.

The rest, I return to the box and replace the lid. I get up, tuck my chair under the table, slide the box under my arm, pick up the loose pictures, and exit the room.

Lolly is at the front desk. Looking at the time, I notice the library will be closing in a few minutes. This library doesn't have evening hours. The patron she'd been checking out heads for the door.

I slide the box toward her and hand her the stack I want copied. "Is it possible for me to get these copied yet this afternoon?"

"Sure," she replies. "It'll just take me a minute." She grabs the box with her other hand, retreating into the private area where the desks are situated and where the copy machine sits. This library is too small to have a machine out in the main area where patrons can access it.

A minute later, she appears with several sheets of paper, handing them to me. "I noticed the orbs in the one picture."

I look at her with renewed interest. Is she an intuitive? I have so much to learn. If she's got skills, I could learn from her. On my next trip, I want to see what books on the subject are on the shelves that I could check out.

Too new at this and too afraid to ask, I decide that conversation will have to be saved for a later time, too.

"I have some knowledge," she continues, almost as if she read my mind, "But, I'm no expert. Frankly, I'd be scared to stay overnight in your house. Have you had any incidents yet?"

"Yet?"

"Oh, yes. The girls who do/did the regular cleaning—"

"They're still going to do it. I insist."

"Oh, good. Anyway, they always talk about how the smell of lilacs is quite strong and doors swing open on their own. They always leave before it gets dark."

"They believe in ghosts?"

Lolly laughs. "They say they don't, but they don't want to know for sure. If it's true, they might never return to the island."

"Do you know anyone who is an expert?"

"Regarding ghosts? I do. I bet he'd be willing to help. The trust would never let him go through the house, let alone stay there when he once requested." She comes around from behind the counter, leads me to the nonfiction section, and pulls a book off the shelf. By Aiden Grey. It's a book about Michigan's haunted houses.

"Can I check it out?" I ask.

"After we set you up with a card, you can."

While she works on a card, I read the back jacket. Aiden Grey is an author, ghost hunter, and paranormal medium who lives on Drummond Island.

A minute later, I have a new library card and feel like a true resident. Amazing how something as simple as a library card can make me feel like I belong.

She says, "Grey lives in the area, you know."

"That's what the back jacket says."

"He's a local celebrity but you wouldn't know it. Fits right in with everyone else. He's here in the library right now. Doing research in the little room that's next to the one we were in."

I hadn't even noticed there was a second little room.

"Why don't you go back and introduce yourself, and if you could do me a favor?"

"Sure."

"Tell him we're closing. By the time the two of you return up front, I'll have everything else shut down and ready to lock the door."

I grin. "Deal." I step toward the back of the library again. Sure enough, there's a second little room, even smaller than the one I was in, which is probably why I didn't notice it. I knock on the door and open it.

His back to the door, he's hunched over the table, writing in a spiral notebook. He lifts his head and looks my way.

"Hi." I step forward and offer my hand. "I'm Hunter Marshall. I've inherited Harbor—"

"Harbor House." He stands and shakes my hand. Easily a full head taller than me, he has wide shoulders and a firm handshake. "When did you arrive?"

"Night before last."

"And, you've already encountered some strange happenings that you can't explain, so you're telling yourself that you've imagined—"

"How do you know that?"

"Lolly wouldn't have sent you to me, otherwise."

"I'm here to tell you that the library is closing."

Surprised, he looks at his watch. "I was so sure—"

I laugh. "No, you're not wrong." At least he has the good grace to chuckle with me. I like his laugh. And his looks, though with two past serious broken relationships, I'm gun shy. I'm attracted, but it wouldn't be wise to pursue that train of thought. I want to hire him for a specific job. Besides, I learned my lesson back in high school. The one time I had admitted someone was cute, and that I was attracted, Amanda and Mars were ruthless, always teasing me.

"I'm looking for someone with psychic abilities. More than I have. I'm relatively new at trusting my instinct but would love to learn more. Are you psychic?"

He gazes at me for several seconds, then nods. He's listening to his gut instinct. How I know that, I don't know. Is that how I appear to others as I listen to mine?

Taking a chance, I ask, "Were you just listening to—"

"My little voice? Yes, I was. The fact that you could tell means you're more of an intuitive than you realize. You were listening to *your* little voice just now, too, weren't you?"

Not waiting for an answer, he turns and packs up his books and papers.

Did he not wait for an answer because I wasn't sure if I should answer him? "What are you researching, may I ask?"

Sliding everything into his bag, he shoulders it and puts a hand on my back, leading us both toward the door. "The Sinclair family, actually."

I stop and look up at him. "Why?"

"Because of the unsolved murder. It's quite the mystery even after all this time. I heard you'd been found and were coming north, so I thought—hoping actually—that we'd have a chance to meet."

Lolly meets us at the library entrance. "Oh, good, you're together. You both have a lot you can share with each other."

We step outside, and Lolly locks the door behind us, giving us a wave.

"I'm meeting my two friends who came north with me for dinner. Would you join us?" I ask.

"I'd be delighted."

On the short walk to the restaurant where Mars, Amanda, and I agreed to meet, I learn Aiden is a Drummond Island resident, born and raised, thirty-four, and has been dealing with spirits since he was a young boy.

Chapter 27

Amanda

Mars and I are waiting on Hunter, though I'm so hungry, I don't want to wait any longer to order. If she's not here in—there she is.

I frown. Who's that following her? Mars glances at me, and I raise my eyebrows as if to respond with *no idea.*

Even before they're seated, Hunter introduces him as Aiden Grey but then is interrupted by the waitress.

They sit opposite Mars and me as she takes our drink orders.

"So, I was at the library," Hunter begins, "researching the house and the family. Got talking with Lolly Pine—"

"Wait, Lolly Pine?" Mars asks. "Isn't that a tree?"

"The Loblolly yes," she answers. "But, Pine is her married name." She turns to Aiden. "What was her maiden name? I forgot to ask her."

"Forest," Aiden says with a straight face and waits.

I choke on my water, then laugh. "Seriously? For real?"

He grins. "For real. Up here, a sense of humor helps us get through the winter."

Concerned, Mars grabs Hunter's arm. "Oh my god, Hunter. Winter. Did you even consider winters when deciding whether to live up here or not?"

"It was on my list."

"But, you hate winter," he says.

"Maybe I'll learn to like it. After all, winter on an island has got to be a totally different experience compared to Detroit's concrete and snow made dirty with traffic. Besides, Detroit's winters are rather mild considering."

"Considering what?" I ask.

"Considering how much more snow we get?" Aiden suggests.

I turn to Aiden. "So, what are winters like up here? For real?"

"Quiet. Ethereal. Like being in a snow globe."

"And, the blizzards?" Mars asks.

"Brutal when the snow is non-stop, but I've not seen such a storm for a couple decades now. The kind that blows for half a week. Now, we get lots of snow but fewer long-lasting blizzards. Climate change, you know."

"Can we go back to how you met?" I ask. "What makes you so special?"

Hunter gasps. "Amanda!"

"You're my friend," I tell her. "I'm protecting you."

"I don't need that kind of protection!"

Mars cocks his head, his gaze pointed at Aiden. "I know you. You're the author of haunted houses. I saw your recent interview where you were debunking certain shows where ghost hunters spend the night in a haunted house. You're good at busting their secrets. Probably not too popular in their circles."

"I'm not," Aiden replies. "Never was, never wanted to be."

"So, what are your tricks?" Mars asks.

"Stop." Hunter demands, then turns to Aiden. "I'm so sorry. I didn't realize my friends could be so rude."

"I'm rather enjoying myself," Aiden replies. "It isn't every day that we have newcomers, especially doubting newcomers. And obviously," he says, indicating Mars, "a fan of reality TV shows."

"What are we doubting?" I ask.

"More like who," Mars says and adds, "That's there's paranormal activity in that house."

"No, there's not—" I reply.

"Yes, there is," Hunter interrupts. "I didn't tell you guys anything because I figured you'd either laugh at me or become so scared, you'd want to leave right away. I want you to stay."

"What have you seen so far?" Aiden asks.

"Doors opening on their own—"

"Slanted floors," Mars counters.

"Is that what we saw today?!" No doubt my eyes are like saucers. I can't believe what I'm hearing.

"Curtains opening," Hunter continues.

"The wind," Mars answers.

"And, Daisy is barking at nothing," she continues.

"She growls at me all the time!" Mars' indignation is showing now as he makes it all about him. Inwardly, I grin. It's easy to rile him. All I ever have to do is mention Daisy.

"But, she's seeing something," Hunter argues. "Other than Mars setting up my online family tree—subversively, I might add—"

"Secretly," he injects. He's miffed.

Hunter ignores him, not letting him make this about him. She asks Aiden, "What do you know about the house, the family?"

"Beyond what you've learned from what the trust gave you, and what you found in the library today—" he says to me "—what hasn't been recorded is that Frank Darnell was seen in Canada after his jail escape and was tracked to a specific tugboat. That tugboat's dinghy was found floating by Harbor House Island on the Canadian side of the island after the murder. Empty. The tugboat's captain claimed his dinghy had been stolen."

"Was it?" Hunter asks.

"No one knows. That's where the trail went cold. Like Sawyer, Darnell was never seen again."

"Are you saying you believe their spirits are part of Harbor House?" I ask.

Long seconds pass as Aiden and I stare at each other.

He finally answers. "Why not?"

Mars laughs. "Oh, I suppose now you're going to suggest a séance to uncover who's haunting us?"

"Who says they're haunting us?" Hunter asks. "Spirits contact us for a number of reasons."

Mars blinks and sits back. "Wow, when did you become such an expert?"

"I'm not. I'm a novice."

"No, you're beyond novice level," Aiden says.

Hunter stares at Aiden. "I am?"

He nods. "Most definitely. The fact that you're already sensing things—"

"How come Mars and I aren't sensing things?" I ask.

Aiden turns to me. "Do you want to? I don't believe you're interested. You have an agenda that is blocking your senses."

I laugh. "That's rich."

For the first time, Hunter is looking at me in a way she never has before. She always accepted my idiosyncrasies without question. Agenda? Is she doubting me? Why would Aiden use that word? What agenda could I possibly have in coming up here with her?

"I trust you," Hunter says to Aiden. "The same way I trusted these two when I first met them." She looks at us. "Though you'll probably now say I'm too trusting, too naïve."

Neither Mars nor I say anything. I don't think Mars trusts Aiden any more than I do.

"So, what's my agenda?" I ask.

"Time will tell," Mars responds quickly. "With you, time always does tell."

I slap his arm with the back of my hand. Always the comedian. If I did have any kind of agenda, it was hoping to spend some quality time with Mars. And Hunter.

"I want to hire you," Hunter declares. "To find the underlying cause of these strange events. As a handyman, too. So, Lolly says."

"Lolly loves to advertise my services."

"When can you start?" she asks.

Mars and I both stare at her. She's hiring him with no discussion with us? She always talked everything over with us.

"Would tomorrow be soon enough?" he asks.

"Tomorrow would be perfect, and I'd like to invite you to stay on the island with us."

I kick her under the table. She moves her feet back.

"No sense in your having to travel back and forth from the big island to Harbor House," she adds.

"I'll see you then." He rises and grabs his book bag. "It was nice meeting you all, and I look forward to getting to know you more."

He's barely out of earshot when Mars hisses, "Are you out of your mind?! You don't know anything about him!"

"Lolly vouched for him," Hunter replies.

"That's all it took? A librarian's word?"

"Hey, hey, hey," I inject. "Are you saying librarians aren't trustworthy?"

"No—no, that's not what I meant." Elbows on the table, he buries his head in his hands, then straightens with renewed energy. "What I'm saying is having him come stay with us is vastly different from having him just working with us. For you."

"It's not like we're living on top of one another," Hunter explains. "For crying out loud, you guys. I thought you were going to support me in this."

"When did you start getting a backbone?" Mars asks.

He said it so I don't have to.

"I've had one—"

I snort. I can't help myself.

"I do," she continues. "Just because you failed to notice it. Suddenly, you're questioning my decisions? Why? You never questioned any of them before."

"We didn't need to. You make sound decisions when dealing with your parents' deaths and the house and such," I say. "I don't recognize this new you."

"I have no idea what you're talking about. I've always had a dream of having a B&B."

I don't respond. Mars doesn't either. But, I slug his thigh under the table.

Hunter's expression changes. She knows Mars and I are communicating. And, she knows I know she knows.

Chapter 28

Hunter

They're slugging each other under the table.

They don't say anything, and they're not looking at each other either. More like looking past me.

The way their arms are moving—the ones next to each other—they're definitely tapping each other under the table, as in code. What they aren't saying is more important than what they are saying.

How did I not see this before?

I need to be clear that I'm staying and seeing this remodel through. Even though I'm not 100 percent committed to staying forever, I think the house will fetch a much higher price with these updates. Way more money than if I had stayed in Detroit and fixed up my house there before selling it. Far too many buyers who buy big houses want move-in-ready homes. Not a house where they'd have to spend a lot of money making the upgrades themselves. Anyone buying this house will more than likely use it as a vacation home, not as a primary residence. "Look, if either of you want to go home, go. Maybe it's time you two went home. I can do this alone. With Aiden's help."

"I don't want you to do it without us, without me," Amanda says, putting her hand, palm down, in the middle of the table.

"Me either," Mars says, putting his hand on top of hers. "We're in this together. And, we need to be more supportive," he adds, his gaze pointedly on Amanda.

I wait until they're both looking at me. "I need your support in words *and* in deed."

"Okay, okay, I'll be more positive about it all," she says. To me, "Forgive us?"

Now, it feels like the past, the friendship we've always had. Where we'd bicker, then make up. I place my hand on top of theirs. We're a threesome again. "All for one, one for all!" we say together. Heads turn. Quizzical looks directed our way.

They both laugh. I smile, and it's a smile I feel down to my toes. But then, a chill goes down my spine.

Suddenly, everything feels off, and I don't know why. I can't blame it on Aiden because I've been feeling it bit by bit once we crossed the lake water from Drummond Island to Harbor House Island as a threesome. Or, is this about Amanda and Mars? Are they being fake and insincere with me? What aren't they telling me?

Is it both of them or just one of them?

Is it possible that whatever happened a hundred years ago is affecting me now? Is there a genuine ghost that I'm sensing? And, if I am sensing these things, how can I protect myself? Will Aiden be able to give me tips?

If he's been living with these sensations most of his life, he's got to be an expert. I trust that belief. I have to. If not, then I need to trust Amanda and Mars more. But right now, the three of us aren't on the same path, despite the hand ritual we just did.

Soon, they'll be returning to Detroit and continuing with the lives they had before we learned of my ancestry. If I return to Detroit, my life will change completely.

Was delving into my ancestry a mistake?

Chapter 29

Mars

Opening the front door to check on the weather, wondering if it's going to be cooler than it'd been yesterday, I see Aiden docking his boat. I cross my arms and lean against the doorjamb, waiting while he unloads a couple suitcases and starts walking across the yard.

Immediately, he looks up and sees me. He nods, but I don't nod back. I'm not a morning person.

I probably should go down the steps and offer to take one of his bags, but that would require energy I don't have. I haven't had my morning coffee. I'm the first one up, which means the coffee hasn't been started.

Aiden climbs the half-dozen steps and joins me on the stoop, forcing me to step back into the house so that he can enter. Once he's inside, he sets his bags down.

His gaze takes in the full expanse of what he sees, which is a view into the front parlor on the left, a glimpse of the room behind, which is another parlor but acts like a family room, the expansive hall with half a dozen doorways, and on the right a small sitting room and behind it is the dining room with an expansive dining table that could seat twenty easily and a fireplace we can stand in.

A staircase to the second floor sits in the middle of the hallway in front of us. We can walk on either side of it to get to the rooms at the back of the hall. The back wall is the kitchen wall.

We enter the kitchen through the dining room. Day rooms, sitting rooms—I'm not sure how they functioned a hundred years ago. I can see why Hunter imagines this house as a perfect setting for a B&B.

"This is quite the house," Aiden says.

I frown. "You've never been here?"

"No."

Why do I think he's lying?

Hunter would say I'm being too suspicious. She'll get angry if I don't treat him well. "Let me show you your room."

"Great. Thank you."

Just as we ascend the stairs and are on the second-floor landing with Aiden following me, Daisy comes out of Hunter's room, growling and snarling.

Normally, if no one is around and she's growling like this, I stick out my foot to block her from getting any closer. The minute she spots Aiden, though, she wags her tail and goes to him all happy.

Chapter 30

Aiden Grey

The minute I see a white dog appear out of a room and approach Mars with growls and snarls, I stop and wait.

My instincts about Mars are being proven by a dog. Animals know.

It isn't until the dog sees me behind Mars that it stops growling and begins wagging its tail, trotting over to me.

Letting go of my bags, I stoop and scratch its head. It flips onto its back—a girl—and lets me rub her belly. When I straighten, she sits square in front of me, looking up. I laugh, stoop, and pick her up. She licks my face excitedly.

"You must have treats in your pockets," Mars snips.

"What's her name?" I ask.

"Daisy."

"You don't like Daisy?"

"More like Daisy doesn't like me. Just me."

I'm not about to ruffle his feathers beyond what already occurred yesterday at the restaurant. I need him and Amanda on my side if this experience is going to work.

Once Mars shows me my room, I begin unpacking. First, clothes into drawers, and then shoving the suitcase with the duffle bag inside it under the bed.

A knock on the door.

"Come in." I'm unloading my smaller book bag and balancing a pile of pictures, stacking them on the only table in the room. A small round table that stands next to an easy chair, sits between two windows.

"Am I interrupting anything?"

A quick glance reveals it's Hunter. The pictures start spilling out of my hands. Quickly, I toss the ones still in my hands on the table, then stoop to pick up the others.

Swiftly, Hunter is beside me, helping me pick them up. Daisy prances around us, sniffing.

Hunter pauses while holding one picture, staring at it. She turns it and holds it in my direction so I can see it. "Who's this?"

A good-looking man with a straw hat and a toothpick in his mouth, with arms crossed, is leaning against a tree. He's grinning at the photographer.

"Sawyer Van Houten."

"Are those pictures of my family."

"Yes."

"Does the library have copies of them?"

"No. Not yet."

"How did you end up with them?"

"Estate sales, lots of online searches—"

"Any ancestor-type websites?"

"A few. Once I started building my tree, I became intrigued with the trees of others. It's how I first saw your connection to the family."

"What? When? I only found out recently."

Hunter appears genuinely surprised, which interests me. "You didn't know?"

She shakes her head.

"That must have been quite a shock discovering your heritage and inheritance."

"It was. But, I didn't initiate the discovery. Mars submitted my DNA and gave me the results as a birthday present recently."

Something wasn't making sense. How could her DNA have

been submitted if she hadn't sent it in herself? I'd known about the connection for—

Her voice interrupts my thoughts. "Mars says he set up an account in my name. Says it was the only way he could send in my DNA. He turned the account over to me."

"And you've changed your—"

"Yes, he told me to change the password. He didn't want any access to it after that. Did he do something illegal?"

"Technically, yes, according to the website, but it sounds like he was doing it for the right reasons of helping you."

"Well, I'm not so sure it was helpful, learning for the first time in my life that I'd been adopted. That my birth mother had been adopted as had hers, too." She pauses, glancing at the photos in my hand. "Any chance I can see them all?"

"Of course! Here." I hand the stack to her. She sits on the floor and starts spreading them out in front of her, sorting them in some kind of fashion.

I grab the rest of the pictures and sit down beside her. A few seconds later, I understand her sorting method. George, Margaret, and Sawyer are in one area. Others she isn't so sure about are being set aside.

I want to help identify those for her. "May I?"

She hesitates, then nods. I clear a space and put George farthest away from us as I build a family tree on the floor with the pictures. Once I have Margaret and Sawyer side-by-side and under George and Edward, with pictures of the adoptees underneath accordingly, along with the picture I had gotten of Hunter, she becomes more involved. She begins flipping pictures, reading any notes I've made on the back.

"Where did you get my picture? I'm not on the website."

"No, but you do have social media accounts. You'd be amazed how much you can find out about people by searching through various platforms and search engines."

"I forget how public we are now, even though so many believe their lives are still private," Hunter says.

"Nothing is private. For a few dollars, it's easy to get details: family members, addresses, phone numbers, jobs—"

"It's scary."

Once we have the pictures sorted, she questions me about relatives she's never known, wanting to know who's dead, how they died, and more. Having done so much research on her family over the years and wanting to write a book about the family, I know her family as well as I know my own.

"Can I take a picture of this?" she asks.

"I'll do it for you." I get my phone, stand, take a picture, and ask for her email address, which she gives me.

"I shouldn't have done that," she says.

"Why not?"

"I don't know you."

"Yes, you do. I'm the man you hired to help with the restoration of damaged tiles and anything wooden. Besides, your instincts have already told you I'm a good guy."

She grins, but there's more. Something in her gaze draws me in. She has no idea how attractive she is, how desirable she is, and not because she's the missing Sinclair heir.

I was attracted the moment I saw her on Amanda's website. A picture someone had taken of the two of them while she posed on a huge rock on Lake Superior. Amanda was posing much like a model would, but Hunter just sat there, hugging her knees, grinning. Like she is now.

"Besides," I offer. "Lolly recommended me and there's no higher recommendation than that."

Her grin broadens. It's a grin of joy. Will that joy continue once she learns the truth?

Outside of my bedroom's open door, we hear Mars and Amanda in the hall arguing with each other, and then they're entering the room.

"What have we got here?" Amanda asks. She comes around and stands behind Hunter and next to me. I pocket my phone.

"Pictures," Mars quips. He joins Amanda.

"Smartass," Amanda says, slapping him.

"Always aim to please," he replies. "Oh, I get it. It's the family tree!"

Hunter twists her head to look up at him. "You've seen these pictures before?"

"No, but it's easy to see the pyramid you made, with George—whose picture I've seen, along with Margaret and Sawyer's up at the top—and then, you, down here at the bottom. What else could this layout be?"

He and Amanda exchange a quick glance. I notice only because I'm standing off to the side of them and half a step behind them, but Hunter didn't see the exchange because she'd already turned her face away from them. What are they up to?

"Who's ready for breakfast?" Mars asks. "I'm making pancakes."

Amanda and Hunter responded enthusiastically. Hunter gets up and follows them out the door when she stops and turns around.

"Thanks," she says, glancing at the pictures. "That helped a lot. You're helping me feel more like a Sinclair."

"Glad I could help."

"I want to know everything you know."

"Anytime," I say. I mean it, too.

Having seen the pictures, she appears to be in a happier place. Happier than she'd been yesterday.

Chapter 31

Anonymous

There's so much I can't control right now. Too much is getting revealed too fast. I need to slow it down. I need time to search and observe. And, I need time alone so no one will suspect me.

Chapter 32*

Margaret

1922

"Father's been acting nervous lately," I tell Frank. We're alone, sitting on the porch swing, waiting for Sunday dinner to be announced.

The summer days are speeding by quickly.

Mary's lessons of household management have ended, and now we spend the cool mornings with light housekeeping or her teaching me how to cook. Afternoons we sew and after dinner, we either pick produce in the garden for the next day's meals or go for a walk on the beach looking for sea glass and rocks. Our collections have grown.

Sawyer stayed in Sinclair one night before moving to the Harbor House permanently while he works on it. I've been meaning to go back and see what work I could do, but there's been so much to do here.

Sundays are different. Sawyer joins us as we attend church in the building that serves as a school if the traveling pastor is in town. Afterward, we have an enormous lunch that provides us sandwich material for a light evening dinner later. This way the cook gets the rest of the day off after cooking lunch.

After that, we spend time on the porch reading or talking. Sawyer usually returns to Harbor House Island after lunch, and Father joins us if he's in town. Usually when Father's in town, Theodore is, too, so those afternoon discussions are lively. Theodore is a logger who's courting Mary, and they became a couple shortly after our arrival. Mary and Theodore always have their heads together, talking and laughing.

Sometimes, Frank brings and gives a bottle of whisky to Grandfather, stating it's a gift from one of his customers. I never gave those customers a thought, until the Sunday I saw Father appear with the bottle in hand and pass it to Frank, who later said it was a gift. Where was Father getting it? Had Father been supplying Frank the alcohol all this time? It was only then I noticed it was a brown bottle—like the one I had found on the beach.

While I said nothing at the time, I mentioned it to Mary later. She laughed and said I must have misunderstood what I'd seen. It didn't make sense to her why Frank would do such a thing. Or Father either. I want to understand, which is why I'm asking Frank now about Father's nervousness, which has increased lately. I've noticed him looking over his shoulder frequently, when walking down the street.

I glance at Frank. He's looking out at Lake Huron. Grandfather's porch has a magnificent view of the lake, the dock, and Harbor House Island. The overgrowth in front of Harbor House has been cut, and the house can be seen again from here.

"No idea what he'd be nervous about," he says, still staring.

Something has captivated his attention. I turn to look. Two boats, looking more like tugboats than anything else, are out past Harbor House Island. Yet, there are no cargo ships nearby.

"Wish I had Grandfather's binoculars that are at the island house. Then, I'd be able to see them better."

Frank turns his head toward me. He's frowning. Then, he smiles broadly. "They must be dusty."

"Actually, no. Mary and I were looking through them at some birds nesting in the trees."

"When was this?"

"That first day I took Mary to the island. I'm going back over tomorrow to see Sawyer's progress. Now that you mention it, it is peculiar that they weren't dusty, seeing how no one had been over there in years."

"Do we really want to live on the island once we're married?" he asks.

His words have the same icy cold effect as diving into Lake Huron in early spring. I drop my hand and jump up from the swing. It zigzags crazily. I take a step away. He reaches out and grabs my hand, stopping me. I look down at his hand, then at him.

I'm irritated. This is the first time he hasn't expressed enthusiasm about our living there. Has he been lying to me all this time?

"It's what we've been talking about all this time, and now, suddenly, you're changing your mind?"

"I'm just concerned for your safety, that's all."

"What dangers are you envisioning?"

Mary comes out and tells us dinner is ready. She pauses and looks at us oddly. She's slow to withdraw, frowning. Why is she concerned at seeing us disagree?

"Let's go eat." I don't want to talk about it anymore. I'm doing it again. Avoiding unpleasantry. I did it all the way through school and have been doing it more than I want since coming back home. Is it because of Mary, how she teases me when I want things a certain way?

He rises, pulls me into his arms, and tries to kiss me, but I give him my cheek instead.

When I pull away, he smiles, but the smile doesn't reach his eyes. He tucks me under his arm as we take the few steps across the porch.

When he releases me so I can enter the house, I can't shake

off the feeling of having been freed. I'm still puzzled and hurt that he's no longer enthusiastic about living on the island.

In the dining room, Frank stops at the sideboard and picks up the brown bottle I had brought back from the beach, having finally washed it out and rinsed the sand off. It was hidden behind flowers that were freshly picked and displayed. Only vegetables are left in the garden now.

Soon, Mary will be returning to Detroit.

"What's this?" he asks, his brows together as he spins it around, studying it.

"We found it on shore," Mary replies.

"Which shore?" he asks.

"Does it matter?" I ask.

He shrugs and sets it down. "No. Not really. Just curious. That's all."

Mary laughs. "Harbor House Island's shore."

Were they messaging each other? What am I missing?

After church, lunch is a strange affair. Father and Theodore are missing, so Frank regales us with amusing stories of banking while in Detroit. Mary tells us she got a letter today from her mother and shares her family's activities. I notice Grandfather stirring the food on his plate. Either he's not feeling good or preoccupied about something—business related, no doubt.

"Are you feeling all right?" I ask him.

He perks up and replies that everything is fine, but I notice he retires to his den rather than spending time on the porch.

Later, after an early supper, I say goodnight to Frank while Mary removes the dishes. Since Grandfather didn't join us, I take a tray into his office.

A few minutes later when I reenter the dining room, the table's been cleared. I notice the brown bottle is gone. Must be it was picked up with the dishes and returned to the kitchen.

Chapter 33*

Margaret

I wake up just before daybreak, unable to go back to sleep. I throw a shawl around my shoulders and go out onto the porch. Through the light slips of fog, I see Sawyer loading his rowboat. He must have come ashore last night or earlier this morning. But then, I see a light shining from what used to be Grandmother's bedroom. The light disappears and reappears again. A signal? But to whom?

I notice Sawyer is still busy loading the boat, but he pauses slightly seeing it, pretending he didn't and continues loading.

Then, I see Father walking away from a bigger boat at the dock with a lantern in his hand.

That's when Sawyer sees Father, who hasn't seen Sawyer. Sawyer looks toward the house. The light is gone. He finishes loading his boat but keeps looking at the island.

Nothing is making sense.

Not having been back to the island since the day Mary and I visited, I decide to row over myself. I want to see Sawyer's progress. I should have been going over regularly, but every Sunday when Sawyer came to church and lunch, he'd update me on what he was doing. Up until now, I didn't feel I needed to check his work.

Why do I feel like I need to now, suddenly?

Dressed, I escape out of the house undetected. Likewise, I slip through town and past the docks unseen. Finally, I'm at the secret slip that Grandfather and I used when he'd take me out on the lake fishing as a young girl. Sure enough, his rowboat is still there. Tall grasses hide the boat and the slip from anyone on shore. Even in the water, the slip is easy to miss unless you're looking for it.

No doubt Grandfather's still fishing, though I can't recall him being gone from the house for any length of time since I've been back. At least, not long enough to go fishing.

Chapter 34*

Margaret

As I pull up to the island's dock, I look around the immediate grounds, extending my search up to the house for any movement, especially the windows. All is quiet.

I tie off and head for the house.

I climb the front steps and immediately notice that several of the steps have been replaced, as have some of the porch railings and floorboards. Everything has been swept, too.

The bell's rope has been replaced and is secured to a clip on the porch floor.

I grab the doorknob and open the door, which slides open smoothly and quietly. The hinges have been oiled.

Inside, the cobwebs and dust are gone. I see signs of repair everywhere I look.

I make a mental note to order paint so that I can start working on the house myself. I smile at the realization of my dream coming to fruition. I'll be living here soon.

A bang sounds upstairs. Sawyer must be up there working. Reaching the upstairs landing, I hear the bang again. It's coming from the right, where the turret room is located. I go into what was Grandmother's bedroom, soon to be mine. A window is open with a shutter swinging in the breeze, banging against the window and house.

At the window, I reach for the shutter, grab it, and stretch out, locking it in place again. Thankfully, one doesn't need a ladder to latch or unlatch these shutters to the house.

Grandfather was ingenious that way—always thinking ahead. I look out across the lake, knowing this was the window from which I'd seen the light flashing earlier.

I look around the room but don't see anything unusual. Taking a step, my foot brushes against something behind the floor-length drapery. I push it aside and find a lantern. No doubt the one used earlier.

Why hide it? Why leave it here? I look out the window again, this time observing everything more closely. That's when I see Father and another man on Sinclair's shore, each carrying a heavy case of something that's being loaded into the back of a freight wagon already mostly covered with canvas. Together, they finish pulling down the canvas, fastening the corners. I look around. Where are Grandfather's binoculars?

Not seeing them, I focus on the two men again. They shake hands and the other man returns to the boat, similar to one of the tugs I saw earlier, and which is docked down away from all the other boats.

Father steps up onto the wagon wheel and sits on the bench, grabbing the reins. Why is he driving a team rather than using a motorized vehicle? Is he headed somewhere that has no roads? Is he going off-road so he won't be caught?

Is the entire wagon loaded with similar cases? Past images click through my head: tugs coming from Canada, finding a bottle on shore and then it disappearing, Father acting nervous, even Grandfather... Wait, is that why Grandfather gave me the house and island for fear Father could lose it? And now, the business?

Could some of Grandfather's visitors of late concern Father's activities?

I'm worried about Father and Grandfather now, but there's nothing I can do right now. My questions will have to wait.

Another bang sounds, only this one is louder and downstairs. A quick search of the rooms on the main floor reveals no one is here. All the windows are secure.

I go down into the kitchen. Unlike any of the rooms upstairs, this room looks lived in. Dishes have been washed and are draining on the counter. Non-perishable food items sit on the counter, stacked neatly against the wall.

Suddenly, I feel air moving. A breeze.

I turn around. The kitchen door leading to the hall is open a crack. I open the door wider and feel the breeze. The outside door is open, with sunlight illuminating the other end of the hallway. Otherwise, the hall is dark. Once again, the lantern is unlit.

I go down the few steps, and there's a flash of light midway to the outside door, occurring where the floor meets the wall. Another step and the light is gone. Something reflected the light. I stoop to look. It's another brown bottle, like the one I found on the beach.

Suddenly, the hall is dark. I jerk upright and gasp seeing a huge someone filling the doorway and blocking the light. I brace myself again the wall as the bulk steps into the hall.

Sawyer.

I sag in relief. "You scared me!"

A few more steps and he's in front of me. Without his hat holding his hair in place, it spills onto his forehead as he looks down at me. He sweeps it back with his hand but to no avail.

"You knew I was here."

"Yes, but I expected to find you in the house." I point to the locked door beside me. "What's in here?"

"I don't know."

I pick up the bottle. He holds out his hand, and I give it to him. He doesn't look surprised. Why not? "I found a bottle like this one out on the beach. And, this lock looks odd."

"To me too, but I don't have a key. Of all the keys your grandfather gave me, none of them open this door."

"Why not?"

"I don't know. We'll have to ask him. The thing that puzzles me, though," he says a hand running down the door and hinges, "is that this door here appears newer than the kitchen and outside doors."

"It doesn't look all that new."

"The air, humidity, and being open to the elements can age it quickly."

"What do you mean, it being open?" I ask.

Sawyer looks at the outside door, "I found both hall doors open. I was outside looking around."

"You didn't open them?"

"No. Not today."

I glance at the kitchen door and the back door, then at him again. He's frowning.

"I didn't open them," he repeats. He's worried, but then his face is blank, and he shrugs. "I'll work itself out. Let's go upstairs."

I turn and retrace my steps into the kitchen, hearing him shut and bolt the outer door, then follow me into the kitchen and shut that door, but he doesn't lock it. "You're not going to lock it?"

He sets the bottle on the island. "I haven't been, at least not during the day. It's easier using this lower back door than going out the front door. I do lock it at night."

"I saw you bring some supplies over earlier."

His eyes widen slightly as if surprised. "What did you see exactly?"

"Not much. I saw some wood being loaded, but not much

else."

He nods, then turns away. What is he hiding?

He spins around and is holding two apples. He offers me one, which I take. He takes a sizeable bite out of the second one.

I open drawers. "There must be a knife around here somewhere." One drawer sticks a little, then pops open but only a few inches before he brushes my hand aside and closes it quickly, handing me a knife.

I take it, not looking at him. I saw a gun in there. What is it doing here? Had it always been there or did he put it there?

It didn't look old or dusty but shiny and oiled, the way I'd seen Grandfather care for his guns. I'm hesitant to ask any questions. Is Sawyer the danger that Frank was talking about? If so, then why did Frank help Grandfather hire Sawyer?

Nothing makes sense.

I go back up the stairs into the dining room and front rooms, all the while thinking and finishing the apple. Sawyer follows me. He takes my apple core and goes to the front door and tosses both his and mine out the door.

Childhood images flash from memory.

"Are you okay?" he asks.

"Yes," I say slowly, then realize he's staring, concerned.

He takes me around, pointing out what he's completed so far. We talk about finishes, and he's interested in my plans to live there.

"It'll a wonderful summer house for visitors."

"And even better once we update the bathrooms," I state. "I'm eager to try living here year-round."

We're in Grandmother's bedroom now, and I'm looking out the window. "I saw a light from this window this morning." Purposely, I turn to see his reaction. There is none, other than a quick glance at the curtain that hides the lantern. But then, his gaze goes toward the other side of the window and its curtain. Does he know about the lantern or not?

"Could it have been a reflection of the sun?" he asks.

There'd been no sun. He has to know that when I saw him it was pre-dawn, the sun just about to rise. What game is he playing? "That must have been it," I say. "Silly me. Imagining things."

"Sometimes things don't appear to be what we think they are," he says.

Chapter 35

Hunter

Present Day

After breakfast, I return to my room to make my bed and finish unpacking. I've been slow in completing the job.

At the window, I open it, welcoming the slight breeze, but close the lightweight opaque curtains simply because I like how they billow in the breeze.

I turn and go to the chest at the end of the bed where my suitcase is open. Picking up a stack of shirts, I move to the dresser. Shirts in the drawer, I close it, and turn to get more clothes.

I freeze.

The curtains are open.

I shut them. I know I did.

The scent of lilacs is in the air.

The rocking chair begins to rock.

No one else is in the room.

The curtains billow, framing the open view.

The rocking chair stops suddenly, as if someone got up.

I want to believe it's the slight breeze that brought in the scent of lilacs, but that's impossible. The flowers aren't in bloom and haven't been for months. I wish Aiden were here. Maybe he could explain. I wish I knew more.

A loud knock on my door surprises me. I jump.

"Hunter?"

Mars' voice.

Suddenly, the scent is gone.

I go and open the door.

"What would you like done with—" He looks at me quizzically. "Are you okay? You look...different. Strange. Like you've seen a ghost. Not okay."

I hesitate. Do I say anything? A little voice tells me not to. "I'm okay. Just busy unpacking. Wondering if I brought the right clothing. You know how Michigan weather changes throughout the day."

He laughs. "Layers. I'm always preaching layers. But, does anyone ever listen to me?"

He continues his usual rant, and I tune him out.

Suddenly, I sense another presence. I turn my head, scanning the room. Daisy sits in the middle of the room, looking up at me, wagging her tail.

"Hunter?"

I turn back to Mars.

"Did you hear me? Aiden's looking for you. He'd like you to—"

"Meet me on the dock." Aiden appears behind Mars. "I thought I'd come up and get you myself."

My mind is flying in so many different directions. "Okay."

Mars turns and starts walking away.

I see something on the floor at my feet. A toothpick. I stoop and pick it up. "Mars, you dropped this." I hold it out.

Mars returns and takes it, though I notice he's frowning at it before putting it in his pocket.

"Actually, that's mine," Aiden says. Mars pulls it out of his pocket and hands it to Aiden. "Sorry about that. Forgot I wasn't in my own house. I'll have to be more careful."

Aiden uses toothpicks too? What is it with these guys?

"I'm used to it," I say, nodding toward Mars who laughs.

Mars leaves.

"I'll meet you at the dock in a minute," I tell Aiden. "I just have something I need to finish."

He leaves.

There's nothing to finish. It's an excuse. I have never felt like this before. Confused. Curious. Intrigued. And cautious, all simultaneously. Just minutes earlier, I had wanted him here and poof, there he was. So, why didn't I say anything?

What is this house doing to me?

Or, is it Aiden himself? Once Mars left, Aiden's aura crashed into mine. I could swear the air is still sizzling and crackling.

But what or who was that unseen presence near me just before Aiden arrived?

Chapter 36

Hunter

Minutes later, I follow Aiden to the dock. He's sitting at the edge, his feet in the water. I haven't done that since I was a kid, so I join him. Even though the water is cold and I'm wearing a thin jacket, it feels good. Quickly, my feet get cold, but I'm not cold.

We sit side by side, neither of us saying a word. The blast of a cargo ship draws our attention to the north. A container ship, heading south is about to disappear behind Harbor House Island. A sailboat had gotten too close to it, hence the horn.

Sounds from Sinclair's dock drift over us. A dragonfly buzzes close by, so close I could reach out and grab it. Ripples in the water reveal active fish. Probably grabbing at bugs sitting on the water. For the first time since I arrived, I feel myself relaxing.

"You're getting grounded."

"I'm sorry. What?"

"What you're experiencing," he says.

The sun comes out from behind the clouds. I squint at the water's bright reflection, wishing I'd brought my sunglasses. Or, wore a hat, though I don't have any. I need to get one.

"Are you saying I'm not grounded enough?"

"None of us are. It's because of the noise that surrounds us. The traffic, the people. We're picking up vibrational signals and don't realize it."

"You mean like radio, TV—"

"And, phones. Yes. Invisible rays of energy. It's how we're able to pick up messages from those on the other side, too. It's all vibrational energy."

Did he somehow know of my earlier experience with the curtains, the rocking chair, and Daisy wagging her tail at nothing?

"It isn't nothing," he adds.

I stare at him. The corners of his mouth lift, and his eyes dance. "You're easy to read. Up there in your bedroom, something was occurring, and Mars interrupted it."

I nod. "And, the toothpick?"

He hesitates, then says. "It's not mine."

"But—"

"It wasn't Mars' either."

"What?"

"It's Sawyer's."

"You mean it's been missed all these years?"

"No."

Goosebumps.

He watches me. As if waiting.

"You mean—"

"He—Sawyer—left it just now. It wasn't there when you opened the door to Mars. I wasn't that far behind him. I notice things. Little things. Things that others miss... I saw it appear."

"That's crazy."

"That's why I wanted to meet you down here to talk. Out here where I know they can't hear us."

"But sound travels—"

"Over water, yes, but have you noticed how you can't hear the words," he says, pointing to Sinclair's docks. "from those who aren't facing us?"

I listen. I'm noticing who I can hear and those I can't. He's right. Anyone facing away from us, we can't hear words clearly at all. It's more like a rumble, a mumble. Even so, we can hear their tone. It's easier to hear higher voices than those with a lower tenor too.

We're sitting with our backs to the house. Close together, our thighs and upper arms nearly touching. And, we're talking in a near whisper. Amanda or Mars would have to be right behind us if they wanted to hear us. And, we're talking low enough that our words wouldn't be traveling across the lake.

Did Aiden choose this position by design? Is he trying to warn me without saying the words?

But, what about the toothpick? How could Sawyer have dropped it just now? Is there a time limit on how long a spirit can remain in our world?

I have so much to learn.

Just as I'm thinking I need to return to the library and chat with Lolly, my phone pings. Pulling it out of my pocket, I have a text from the library, telling me I have books ready for pickup. Using our state's library inter-loan system, Lolly has found additional books she thought I'd like to read.

I'm excited, more than ever now about the material, hoping I can learn more details about my family. More details than even Aiden knows. Though, there's no reason he couldn't have read the same books. Truthfully, I have no idea how much he knows. "Are there things about the family that you haven't revealed yet?" I ask. "Things I don't know?"

I need to stop blurting out my thoughts. No, I need to ask the questions, to stop holding everything in.

"That's hard to say. I've only been here one night."

"True. But, that wasn't the question I was asking."

It feels like we've been friends for years rather than just a couple of days.

Strangely, I feel safe with him. So, if I feel safe, why do I doubt myself?

"How would you feel about holding a séance?" he asks.

"With the four of us?"

"No, just you and me to start with. I get the impression your two friends wouldn't be open to the idea. In fact, I suspect they'd try to talk you out of it the first chance they get."

"Can I think about it?"

"Sure." Moving his feet out of the water, he stands and holds out a hand to help me up. He pulls me up, not letting go until I'm standing solidly on my own two feet again. I shiver.

Not out of fear but out of wonderment and feeling the electrical and vibrational change between us. Who is this man, this Aiden Grey?

Why do I suspect he has secret abilities that not even the locals don't know about or recognize?

Chapter 37

Hunter

"Sawyer Van Houten was not a good guy."

I stare at the woman who just checked out my books. Why would she say such a thing? She's older than Lolly, long past government retirement age. Do they allow volunteers behind the desk up here? They didn't in Detroit. Volunteers were relegated to busywork that librarians didn't have time to manage, like dusting, cutting out materials for kids' crafts, and checking shelves for books not shelved correctly. Most of the libraries I knew, at least those of any size, relied on their volunteers.

Were volunteers more valuable in this small community? I'll have to ask Lolly the next time I see her.

In the meantime, I'm stuck with this Negative Nellie. "How do you know that?" I'm highly curious now because of her profound statement, especially given how others have said otherwise.

"Because he left Margaret when she needed him most."

She sounds like one of those old natty spinsters in a Dickens novel. If others don't live by her standards or rules, then they're not worthy of existence. She'd probably even question Margaret's diary where Margaret says Sawyer was sweet and kind. Never coming home without a gift. A wildflower. Freshly baked cookies from her grandfather's cook. Beach glass. Shells. Special rocks. A doodle he'd made on the back of some business paper. Or, just a sweet note or short poem he'd written.

Sawyer was a romantic, a man totally in love. Yet, what did I really know about him? I had only Margaret's say-so. And her grandfather's, who had turned over his business to them both.

"Rumor has it," she continues, "that he walks the grounds at night and by day is trying to get revenge."

"Revenge for what?"

"No one knows."

I chuckle aloud.

That was a mistake.

Her brows come together in a deep, punishing frown. I push away an image of her practicing black magick.

I blink several times to make the vision vanish. Now, she sneers at me in a smiling way. "You'll see." She pushes my checked-out books toward me. "You do know they never found his body? He left her."

"Yes, I know." I open the book bag I brought, prepared to slide the books in.

"He loved his toothpicks," she says, pulling out the book at the bottom of the pile. Flipping a few pages, she finds what she's looking for, opens the book fully, then twists it around one-hundred eighty degrees so that I'm looking at two pages of pictures. One of Harbor House. Another of the shed, looking as if it was newly built. Had Sawyer built it? And, then on the opposite page, a picture of Sawyer, his arms crossed, leaning against a tree.

With a toothpick in his mouth.

The same picture I'd seen in Aiden's pile.

I know I had asked him where he'd gotten the pictures, but what had he said? Why couldn't I remember?

I close the book and look at the cover. Written decades ago, with no author's name.

She takes the book from me and reaches over to slide it into my bag. I take charge of the chore and push it and the rest of the books into the bag myself. I'll have to investigate the book further later, along with Aiden's picture.

Once again, she's talking. Somewhere along the way, I stop listening. Thankfully, she's going on about some other family in the region, saying how the early relatives were all crooks and thieves, highly engaged in the bootlegging operation that had operated within Sinclair's company without him even knowing it. Him who? George? Sawyer? Eddie? The woman is lousy with her pronoun usage. Who's she talking about now? George Sinclair, or is she back to Sawyer?

Do I dare interrupt and ask? I think not.

Weary of her voice, I find a spot where she's pausing, where I can interrupt without appearing rude, and thank her.

I'm eager to get home and explore the books, but I want to talk with Aiden privately. I'm overthinking my doubts, not sure anymore what they entail.

On the boat ride home, however, I'm rethinking my idea of talking to Aiden right away. I need to arm myself with the information these books will provide. A little distance plus added data will allow me to better judge if he's telling the truth about what he knows.

Once I'm inside the house, I find Aiden hard at work, modernizing one of the bathrooms and doing a spectacular job. It's more important to get the rooms modernized than it is to satisfy my curiosity. His being busy confirms my need to wait. I'll do my research first. My questions can wait.

Chapter 38

Hunter

When I go into the kitchen with the few groceries Amanda asked me to pick up, I find her making a pie. Yesterday, she found some blueberry bushes out back and picked enough for a cobbler, but then we convinced her to do a pie. She's famous for her baked goods.

After putting the groceries away while she puts the decorated top crust on the pie and pops it in the oven, I pour two tall glasses of iced tea.

"You're going to do this aren't you?"

"I haven't decided."

"Yes, you have. I can tell. You're falling in love with this house more each day. I can see it."

I was. We'd only been here a few nights, but it feels longer. Almost as if I had never lived elsewhere. "You think I'm making a mistake by not selling everything here?"

She hesitates. She's taking her time replying.

Finally, she asks, "Don't you want to go back to Detroit?"

"To what? My garage and outdoor porch were destroyed. I have no job and no home."

"I didn't mean right this minute. Maybe in a few weeks? As if this were a vacation? Won't you miss Detroit?"

"The hustle and bustle? The noise? The crush of people? The insane traffic?"

She laughs in acknowledgment, as we've both complained about those things often enough. "But what about the museums, the restaurants, the events?"

"We haven't been to an event...in how long? Plus, everything is more expensive. Really, what am I going to miss?"

"Me? Us?"

"Oh, Amanda." I hug her. Has she been relying on me all these years without my realizing it? "We can always chat via text or video messaging."

She sighs. "I know. But, it just won't be the same."

"Nothing ever is. Look at how quickly I lost my parents and just recently my house."

"But you didn't lose it."

"To fix it and stay there would cost me my savings, which means I'll never get my B&B unless I win the lottery."

"There's always a chance."

"And, that's what this is. A chance. An opportunity. I'd be foolish not to take it. To take a path I never realized was an option."

"I suppose."

She stands there looking lost. She still has Mars.

Or does she? Is there something going on between the two of them that I don't know about? What is she so afraid of?

"I can't imagine leaving everything behind like you're doing." She scans the room, and I try to see it through her eyes. She's all about functionality, which this kitchen isn't. Not yet, anyway. And, like Mars, she doesn't like being unorganized. Not that I do either, but she gets horribly uptight about changes.

"Does Mars think I'm making a mistake?" I ask.

She rolls her lips inward, then focuses her attention on finishing the cleanup she started while we were talking.

She wants to say something but is holding back. Why? Her change of focus from me to cleaning is a direct attempt to not answer my question.

BANG!

We jump and turn to the sound that's coming from behind the closed kitchen door to the outside hallway.

Slowly, the door creaks open.

Fingers appear, grabbing the door.

Amanda screams, "What the—"

Mars steps halfway into the room.

"Don't do that to us!" she cries out.

"Do what?" he says, fully in the room now.

I laugh out loud and should instantly regret doing so based on the glare Amanda gives me, but I don't. I had nearly screamed, too, but now it's just funny. "Scare us," I answer. Obviously, the house is getting to us. "What caused that loud bang?"

He reaches down and reveals an empty pail from behind the door. "I'd been washing some walls and decided to dump the dirty water outside rather than take a chance with the current plumbing system. I hit the door with it accidentally."

His slight grin tells me it wasn't accidental at all.

Had the back door been unlocked all this time? Why am I even questioning if it was locked? People are working in the house. Of course, it's been unlocked.

Chapter 39

Amanda

Both Mars and Hunter leave the kitchen, and I'm stuck alone with my thoughts. I seem to be stuck alone a lot. I don't like being alone. I hate the thought I'm not in a relationship. I was always keen on Mars, but I'm stuck in the friend zone with him. Always have been. When I get back home, I need to find some new hobbies that involve men. I wonder if I should start playing golf. Become helpless on the course and ask for some tips. Would I appear stupid to the other players?

I hate how no one takes my opinion seriously. Coming up here, I was hoping to spend quality time with Hunter and hopefully get some one-on-one with Mars. Who am I kidding? He's never going to see me as anything but a buddy. Like Hunter. But now, Hunter's getting all the attention. I feel like a third wheel.

It was horrible how her parents died, murdered like that. I get how Mars was paying more attention to her at that time, but it's almost as if he's never stopped. And then, he gives her a birthday present that turns her life upside down. She's practically royalty up here. The Sinclair name is everywhere. And, *then,* that storm changed everything again!

I hate the thought of losing her as a friend. Does she seriously think we can be close if we're separated by 400 miles? A video call isn't my style.

Chapter 40

Hunter

After I leave the kitchen, I search for Aiden and find him upstairs with another man he introduces as Danny Buchanan, the man Aiden tells me I want to hire as my contractor if I'm serious about remodeling the bathrooms and kitchen and getting the job done quickly. Aiden has done well so far by himself, but with Danny, the job will get done much faster.

They're talking about how they grew up together, and Aiden is saying that everything he knows about home repairs, he learned from Danny.

"Oh, I'm serious, about the remodel," I say. "I just haven't run that bell yet." Despite having said that, I know I'm going to move forward with the improvements. No more dillydallying. I also know that I won't be returning to Detroit no matter how much Mars and Amanda try talking me out of staying.

This house feels right, which makes little sense considering how my parents' home had always felt like home. Safe. And yet, they'd been murdered there.

As if this one is safe with all the strange things that are happening. A murder took place here, too.

The difference between these two homes is that I feel safer here, but I don't know why. Is it because I'm changing and feeling differently, no longer the person I was in Detroit? That I'm connected even though I'd been abandoned through the generations.

Just then, Aiden pauses, looks at me, really looks at me, and smiles. Then, he turns away and becomes engaged with Danny again.

What was that look about? No way he can read my thoughts. Or, can he? No, he can't. Impossible. But, he sensed something though.

I listen to them for a minute, then inject myself into their conversation, wanting to know more about the plumbing updates that will be required. Then, as we move around the second floor, Danny talks about the wiring, and Aiden tells him how he and the man working with him have been rewiring the house, including updating the circuit breaker box.

"Can we look at the attic," Danny asks.

"Certainly." I say. "Though. I don't even know where it is."

"The door is in the hallway," Aiden says.

"It is?" I'm surprised.

Aiden leads Danny and me midway in the hall and pushes on a part of the wall that has one hanging picture but no furniture in front of it. Magically, a door opens.

I gasp. "How did you know it was there?"

Aiden just smiles.

Then he shrugs his shoulders and says, "It's a gift. I know old houses."

But, how does he know *this* one so well?

Danny pulls a flashlight out of his tool belt and turns it on, flashing it up the unpainted wooden stairs. "All these old houses have secrets. Staircases, rooms, hideaways."

My gaze follows the beam. I follow Danny up the stairs, and Aiden follows me. The attic is humongous, and even the ceiling is high. Surprisingly, the attic isn't hot or dusty despite all the stuff that's stored up here: furniture, chests, pictures, and more. Has the attic been cleaned regularly like the rest of the house over the years?

I can't believe that a cleaning here amounted to anything more than getting rid of spiderwebs and dust.

Suddenly, I feel a light breeze. Looking around, I notice there aren't any windows, just a few vents here and there that appear slatted and open. That's strange.

Am I becoming paranoid about any hint of a breeze inside the house, believing it's paranormal?

I ask, "How is it I'm feeling air moving?"

"Soffit vents," they say at the same time.

Danny explains how the vents work and finishes with, "The house is sound. Remarkably so considering how long it's stood empty."

"The trust took good care of it," Aiden says.

"Appears so," Danny says.

Back on the second-floor hallway, I tell Danny, "I want to hire you. When can you start?"

He and Aiden exchange glances. Did Aiden just give him a slight nod? Immediately, Danny says, "Would the day after tomorrow be too soon?" He tells me his price.

I shake his hand, giddy with excitement. I can't believe I've made a decision this big without mulling it over for several days or making my infamous pro-versus-con list.

Who am I? What unknown forces are influencing me?

Danny asks permission to take measurements now and bring samples of material back later after dinner, telling me it will take a couple days for materials to arrive once ordered. Tomorrow they start the prep work.

I agree.

Aiden goes with Danny, and together they measure the house.

A bit later, I'm waiting for Aiden by the front door with a file in hand.

He smiles, seeing me waiting for him.

A feeling of being safe washes over me, which is strange because all I want to do is ask him about the picture I saw in the library that's also in his collection.

Am I receiving a message of some kind?

He stands in front of me. "To what do I owe this pleasure?" he asks.

"Let's go into the parlor." Once we're seated, I get to the point quickly. "I was at the library the other day and got some books." I pull out the book, find the bookmark, open it, and hand it to him. "Do you recognize this picture?"

He stares at the picture: Sawyer shouldering against a tree, arms crossed, and a toothpick in his mouth. A corner of Aiden's mouth twitches and the outer edge of an eyebrow goes up. Yup, he recognizes it.

"I do," he finally says.

"It's in your collection."

He nods.

"It's a book with no author. Isn't that odd?"

He continues staring at the picture. "Probably a local group or someone who published it gave it to the library."

"It doesn't even have a copyright." I show him the copyright page.

"Not totally unusual back in those days. Especially, if privately printed. It's an old book."

"Who would do that around here?"

Is there a reason why he isn't looking at me? Does he know anything about the author of this book?

Aiden's electrician calls out his name, and Aiden responds. "In here."

Minutes later, Aiden leaves with him to look at a problem encountered in one of the new bathrooms.

I sit there alone, looking through the book at pictures Lolly says were family members or were associated with the mill.

Why do I get a sense that Aiden was about to tell me something important? Something he's been hiding all this time? And if that's true, how can I still feel safe with him?

I'm not solving anything sitting here wondering. Maybe over time, as Aiden becomes more comfortable, he'll relax and reveal—what? As much as he says he was an open book when we first met and appeared as such when meeting with Mars and Amanda, he's holding back information. Why?

Chapter 41

Hunter

The day has been long but satisfying.

I'm happy here.

Truthfully, I made my decision to stay here upon learning of my inheritance. So, why do I continue to hem and haw about it? Because I'm nervous about the winters? About being isolated after a lifetime of being surrounded by noise and people?

Of all things I should be nervous about, I should be nervous about all of these unexplained happenings, but strangely I'm not.

Maybe after the house is updated, and I've done more research and can learn what it will take to run a small business here, I'll be more comfortable with my decision to stay in this house.

Getting ready for bed, my worries don't stop. Can I earn a satisfactory living here? Will enough people want to use this island as a vacation getaway? Can the house sustain a business such as I envision? If it works for Mackinac Island, why can't it work here? Granted, the Island doesn't have activities like a golf course, horses, bicycles, and shops, but Drummond Island does.

If I decide not to stay, I can at least sell everything here—business, island, everything—and either purchase an already up-and-running B&B or start new in a more favorable location. I don't *have* to return to Detroit. I can buy property anywhere.

But honestly, this location...how could anyone *not* want to vacation here? There's so much to do on Drummond Island. Michigan is a fun, recreational state. Winter or summer.

I climb into bed and plump up the pillows, stacking them against the headboard, and lean back against them. I open Margaret's diary.

Every day I'm with Sawyer, I'm thankful that I didn't marry Frank. Had he been with Mary all along?

So, Margaret worried and questioned things, too. A comforting thought knowing we shared that trait.

I never got a chance to meet Frank's family, but I remember him talking about an older sister who he described as beautiful with a bright future until she became pregnant and was kicked out of the family home. The way Frank spoke about her, he obviously adored her and was devastated when she became destitute, giving birth to a boy. Named Antonio, I think he said. Apparently, Frank had to convince the family to take Antonio in when his sister died a couple of days later from childbirth.

So many women died giving birth.

I'm frightened at the thought of giving birth. We're here alone on this island, and while there's a doctor on Drummond Island, he doesn't live in Sinclair. He lives on the other side of Drummond. Do all women have this fear?

A soft breeze ruffles the curtains slightly. The scent of lilacs fills the air.

Daisy, who'd been stretched out by my leg, raises her head.

The rocking chair begins to rock, with the curtains billowing again. An icy wind sweeps past me.

The lilac smell disappears, and the chair stops rocking. Instantly.

Daisy stands, planting her legs as if in attack mode, barks, then growls.

I freeze, my gaze darting around the room, waiting and wanting to see something. Dreading what I might see at the same time.

I hear footsteps outside my door.

I throw back the cover and rush over to the door on tiptoes. As quietly as I can, I open the door and peek out.

No one is there.

I stick my head out the door and look to the right and then to the left.

No one there.

I hear a rattle. My heart racing, I step into the hall. The secret door to the attic is open just enough that I can see it hasn't been closed properly.

I move toward it, then hear the rattle again. The sound is up above me.

Someone is in the attic.

Should I go find a flashlight? Will I be safe if I investigate it myself?

Goosebumps dance along my arms and spine. The hair on the back of my neck tingles.

Instinct tells me I'm safe. But, fear in the form of goosebumps and raised hairs is telling me otherwise.

Slowly, I open the door, remembering how it creaked before. Strangely, this time there are no creaks. Did someone oil it?

I creep up the stairs, taking one at a time, almost crawling up them, and stop at each step to listen. At the point where I can peer into the attic with my eyes at floor level, I stay there, sweeping my gaze from one end to the other.

A shadow moves in one corner. Someone with a flashlight.

Mars!

Still in stealth mode, I continue up the stairs until I'm standing on the attic floor itself, then shout, "Mars!"

He screams, turns, and fumbles the flashlight, catching it before it hits the floor.

"You scared me! What are you doing?"

I repeat his question back to him. "What are *you* doing? Why are you up here this time of night? Why are *you* being so sneaky?"

"I'm not—I mean—okay, yes, I am. I thought I saw some wallpaper when we were up here earlier. I couldn't go to sleep until I checked." Immediately, he comes toward me. "Probably better to check during daylight hours."

"You think? Why didn't you just turn on the overhead light?"

He shrugs his shoulders, but his expression doesn't match the shrug. What is he hiding? Why is he really up here?

"Come on, let's go back to bed," he says.

Why do I think he hasn't been in bed yet? Because he isn't in pajamas? Because he's still wearing the jeans and shirt he wore earlier?

Mars follows me back downstairs, tells me goodnight, and goes down the opposite hall to his room. He doesn't even glance my way as he enters his room and shuts the door.

What doesn't he want me to know? What is he hiding?

Back in my room, I shut the door, and stand with my back to the door, leaning on it.

The lilac scent is back.

The rocking chair moves again. Only this time, there's no breeze moving the curtains.

Daisy sits near me, her head cocked one way, then another as she stares at the rocker.

Someone is here.

But who?

"Margaret?" I whisper.

She *is* here. I can feel her smiling. The rocking continues in an easy, slow manner.

And then, suddenly, it stops.

She's gone.

The cold has returned.

Daisy stands in the middle of the room, staring at the corner that had her growling before.

The cold evaporates.

Daisy snorts and circles a couple times before finally lying down on the floor, facing the corner.

"Not going to sleep in your own bed?" I ask.

She gives me a soft yip, then closes her eyes.

I wish sleep could come that easily to me, but my head is filled with too many unanswered questions right now.

I slide under the sheet again, pick up Margaret's diary, turn the page, and ignore that the chair is rocking again, slowly, and almost purposefully.

The lilacs have never been this beautiful. Grandfather told me it was spring with lilacs blooming when Grandma died. I wish I could have known her, but she died just before I was born. My father was raised here, yet I never heard him talk about it.

Turning another page, there's a picture, a self-portrait I assume, of a little girl sitting inside the large lilac bushes that appear to be a bit bigger than she is, but not by much. A secret hiding space.

I wonder if Margaret's self-portrait was a memory of herself as a little girl when she'd visited the island or an imagined memory she had wished for. While growing up, the house had been vacant. From everything I've read so far, after George's wife died, it doesn't appear he ever visited the island again. Had Margaret snuck over here a time or two when she was little? Because she was transported to Detroit's boarding school when she was six years old, I doubt she could have been physically capable of rowing from Sinclair to Harbor House Island on her own.

"Didn't you hear me knock?" Amanda's head is poking into the room.

I must have been lost in my reading. "Come on in," I say.

Amanda takes a couple steps and stops, pointing at the moving chair. "Wha—what—?"

The rocking stops. One curtain billows. Thankfully, the window is open, even though there is wind outside.

"It's drafty in here," I say. Why do I feel the need to defend what we're seeing?

She glares at me. "I'm not stupid. There's no wind moving the other curtains." She spins around, stepping toward the door. "I can't do this."

The door clicks shut behind her.

I run after her, hoping to convince her otherwise.

I crash into Aiden instead. His arms go around me to keep me from bouncing backward and falling. Stunned at the intimate embrace—even if only for a nanosecond—I turn around and return to my room. Aiden follows me.

Seeing the diary on my bed, he picks it up. "I didn't realize she had a diary."

"Mars and Amanda know of it, but they haven't seen it."

"May I?"

I nod, knowing he's asking permission to read it.

He reads a few pages. "I suggest you don't let them read it." Moving to me, he hands me the book. He's so close I have to tip my head back to look at him.

"Why not?"

"No solid reason. Just instinct."

My nod is subtle. He smells so good and looks even better. His eyes, which I thought had been green were green in the center but rimmed with gray.

"Don't you agree?" he whispers.

His breath on my face is a welcoming caress. His lips part slightly as his face inches toward mine, his gaze focusing on my lips.

"Hunter! Why is Amanda so—"

Aiden takes a step back as Mars bursts into my room.

Mars stops, a look of surprise on his face. "OMG, I'm so sorry."

Then he frowns, looking almost angry. No. Agitated. Because Aiden is in my room?

Mars spins around and exits just as quickly as he entered.

"That didn't go well," Aiden says.

Silently, I agree and am glad that Mars didn't see the diary that had been in my hand but hidden in the folds of my long nightgown.

Aiden steps toward the door. "Good night, Hunter. Sweet dreams." The door clicks shut behind him. His footsteps diminish as he walks down the hall to his room. I hear the click of his door, too.

Turning around, I face the room. The rocking chair starts its slow rock again.

Margaret is comforting me.

There's no other explanation. I never feel threatened when the chair rocks or the scent of lilacs is around.

But, if she's the gentle breeze, then what is the colder, harsher breeze that occurred earlier, chasing her away and always makes me feel unsafe? Or, should I be asking *who*?

Chapter 42*

Margaret

1922

I turn and stare at Sawyer. He's staring back. Words spoken in the past taunt me.

Nothing is as it seems.

But, that's not what he just said. He said, *Sometimes things don't appear to be what we think they are*. So, why does it feel the same?

His eyes look familiar. I hear Johnny's voice and then in my mind's eye see Johnny turn and wave at me.

Sawyer frowns and steps toward me, reaching out. "Are you okay? You look like you've seen a ghost." The air sizzles. The hairs on my arms rise.

Before he can touch me, I turn and walk out of the room. Goosebumps everywhere. He follows.

I can't look at him. I'm nearly at the stairs and trip on my own feet. I gasp and reach out for the rail. Instead, a hand grabs mine and pulls me back. I'm thrown against his body, and I cling to him, trying to regain my balance.

His arms wind tightly around me. He takes a step back while still holding me, forcing me to step with him.

Only when we're safely away from the stairs does he loosen his grip. He looks down and brushes the hair away from my face. "You scared me."

"I—I—" I can't find the words. I'm mesmerized by the concern in his eyes as he searches my face.

Johnny.

His lips are on mine, and he's holding me tighter now than he was a minute ago, and my arms wrap around him, holding him just as tightly.

When he releases me, I open my eyes, surprised at the separation.

And then, realization hits. What have I done? My hand goes to my mouth, and I step back.

"I'm so sorry," he says. "I shouldn't have done that."

"I'm not blaming you."

"You should."

I shake my head. I can't. From the first time I spotted him onboard the steamer, his aura has drawn me like a moth to a bright light in the dark. Even now, the air is thick with unrealized emotion.

"I should go home," I say.

He nods.

We go downstairs and out the front door, words unspoken. I want to reach out and hold his hand, but instead, I ball my hands into fists and jam them into the pockets of my trousers.

As we approach the dock and our two boats, he says, "For the time being, it's probably better if you don't come to the island alone."

At first I laugh. "You sound like Frank."

He's not laughing. "It's dangerous."

"You're right. You're dangerous."

I leap into the boat and pick up the oars, pushing myself away from the dock as he throws the rope that was looped around a pier into the boat.

One last look at the island reveals he's still standing there rooted, just like he had been on board the steamer when I first saw him.

I want to row back to him but force myself to further the distance between us instead.

How am I ever going to explain this to Frank?

I'm not.

I can't even explain it to myself.

Sawyer isn't Johnny. He can't be. Johnny would have identified himself.

Chapter 43

Hunter

Present Day

The next day, I meet Mars in the backyard. I just finished painting the extended wardrobe that had been built in my room. I came out to clean my brushes. Mars is cleaning his painting supplies, too, having just finished painting the first bathroom.

I enjoy getting Mars' viewpoint on color. He's got a natural eye for color. I can see why his businesses are growing.

"Are you sure you know what you're doing?" he asks.

I rise from rinsing my brushes, with residue paint dripping onto the grass. "What do you mean? You're helping me with the remodeling—"

"No, I mean about Aiden. What do you really know about this guy?"

"Say again?"

"Seriously, Hunter. You're making quick and rash decisions all of a sudden."

"Rash?"

"You know how it takes you days to decide anything. And, those pro/con lists you make—"

"I'm still making them."

"You are?"

"Just because I haven't been showing them to—"

"But, you've always shown them to me in the past."

"That was the past. This is now."

"That's what I'm talking about. This is a Hunter I don't

recognize."

"That other Hunter died with your birthday present."

He stares at me. I can see different emotions flickering in his eyes.

Surprise.

Confusion.

Remorse?

And then, I'm not sure what emotion I'm seeing. It's as if a veil has dropped, hiding my ability to read him.

"I'm sorry..." he starts. "No, I'm not sorry. Look, I may have been stupid in how I presented you with that information, but I'm glad you know now. How much more awful would have it been had you found out when you turned 60? No one should have secrets kept from them like that. No one."

Secrets. Everyone has them. Including Mars. Didn't he secretly submit my DNA? "About Aiden—"

"I'm sorry I questioned that, too. You're entitled to meet new people. I guess I'm just jealous seeing you two grow close so quickly. It's like I wasn't invited to join the party."

"We're going to do a séance later. Want to join us?"

"Oh, god, no! Knowing there could be ghosts here is frightening enough. Talking to them—are you nuts?!" Finished with his cleaning, he leaves.

I stand there staring out at the lake.

And then, I laugh. Mars can be so superstitious at times. He loves the romanticism of ghosts, but he's right. Not everyone believes in ghosts, let alone wants to converse with them. Once upon a time, I'd been afraid of them. But now, I welcome them. Well, sort of. I'm okay with Margaret's ghost. It's the unknown ones that are scary.

But then again, aren't strangers scary, too, until you get to know them?

Haven't I always wanted this ability without realizing it?

Is that why I find Aiden so attractive? His ability to understand spirits, to communicate with them at will? But then again, when have I ever seen him do that?

So far, all I've seen is—nothing. He talks a lot about his ability, but nothing has happened while he's around.

Well, other than the toothpicks he claims suddenly appeared—the ones I didn't see appearing. How do I know he didn't throw them down himself?

Is Mars right? Should I be suspicious of Aiden?

I'm letting Mars' ideas get into my head. I need to shake them off. I need to make up my own mind. Without undue influence.

Chapter 44

Aiden

After lunch, Hunter and I are alone in the kitchen doing dishes. Earlier, I overheard her inviting Mars to the séance I want to perform and am glad he turned down her invitation. I want this séance to be just the two of us.

I don't want her friends' negative energy to interfere with the spirits. If anyone were to appear, Amanda and Mars could react, showing fear. Energy that could interfere with our trying to discover who they are. Most spirits are just like us—they want to be welcomed. But, I'm wondering if there's one spirit wanting to control or frighten us instead.

"Ready to do the séance after we're done here?" I ask.

"Sure. I'll let Amanda and—"

"I'd prefer it be just you and me," I interrupt. "In fact, can we do it in your room where we won't be interrupted?"

"My room?"

"It's bigger than mine, plus you have a larger table in there already."

"Oh...okay, I guess."

She's nervous. At being alone with me? That no one else will see our results? Or, is it about the spirits themselves? "Would you rather not do it?" I offer.

"No! No. It's not that."

I was washing and she dried, but there's nothing left to wipe. I take the dish towel from her and hang it up to dry. I walk out of the kitchen, and she follows.

"I've never done anything like this," she says.

We head upstairs. I respond, "Doing anything new can be nerve wracking."

She laughs. "True. You're the expert. You wouldn't lead me down any shady alleys, would you?"

This time I laugh. "No. Not for a minute. If I suspect anything's wrong, we'll stop. In fact, if you want to stop at any time, just say the word."

"And what word would that be?"

"Stop."

At her door, I pause, my hand on the doorknob. I wait for her to respond. I can tell she's mulling it over. Probably thinking of all the pros and cons.

And then, she smiles. "Let's do it."

I open the door and step aside so she can go in first. She goes directly to the empty round table by the easy chair and moves it in front of the chair while I grab a straight-back chair that sits in front of a dressing table, placing it opposite the easy chair.

She chooses to sit in the wooden chair, so I go around and sit in the easy chair, sitting on the edge of the seat.

"So, how does this work?" she asks.

"Sometimes, I begin by using a pendulum, oracle, or tarot cards, all of which can answer questions that we ask. Those are tools I use with clients who have no experience or communications with spirits."

"But...?"

"You're already communicating with them. We don't need those tools. It's just a matter of inviting them to converse with us here. Now. At our invitation. Up until now, you've just witnessed their sudden arrivals."

"Their? You think there's more than one ghost here?"

"I do."

Her eyes widen and then the corners of her mouth lift in the smallest of grins. "Really?"

I nod. "Ready to begin?"

She nods.

I put my arms along the outside rim of the table, then turn my hands over so they are palm up. "Put your hands in mine. Make sure your feet are flat on the ground."

She squirms a little, moving her body forward a bit, her spine straight, her hands comfortably lying in mine. I tighten my fingers around hers, and she mimics the handholding.

Her eyes brighten. She wants this. She licks her lips, which distracts me for a minute.

Concentrate, I tell myself while inhaling. I exhale with my eyes closed. My shoulders drop, and I feel a sense of calmness.

Opening my eyes, that sense of calmness turns into sexual energy as she stares at me as I now stare at her, our gazes locked. Is she not feeling the energy that flows between our hands?

She whispers, "Who's here?"

Immediately, the rocking chair rocks. Hunter doesn't realize it, but she's taken control of this séance. The spirits are drawn to her.

"Margaret," she says, turning her head to look at the moving chair and smiles. "She's here almost every night in that chair. It's where she rocks her baby."

"You're that baby."

Startled, her head swivels, looking at me, her lips parted in surprise. "No, I'm not."

"But, you are. Just a few generations removed. "She's protecting you."

"From whom?"

Immediately, a chilly breeze sweeps over us.

"From that," I say.

"Who is it?"

"I don't know. Why don't you ask?"

"It's that easy?"

"Yes."

Her gaze sweeps the area behind me, around me. "Who are you?" she demands.

I'm surprised at her forcefulness. The chair stops rocking.

"Is that normal?" she asks.

"Yes. I suspect you scared them away."

"That's possible?"

"Always. You're in control here. They aren't. They like to think they are, but you can command them to go, to stop any behavior you don't like."

"How is that?"

"Because you're the one fully occupying the space. Your energy supersedes theirs because the bulk of their energy is on the other side. They're able to visit with just a smattering of the energy they once had while here and alive. They're visitors."

"But, we still don't know who or what that cold is about."

"Has it done anything you would call negative?"

"Um...no. It's more like it's been passing through me."

I wait. I want her to think it through. It's the only way her confidence will grow when dealing with ghosts.

She asks, "Do you think it's wanting attention?"

"Possibly."

"How can I find out more about it? About them?"

"I can do a tarot reading. It'll provide characteristics of the event or individual. We're still guessing, but it becomes a more educated guess."

"How do we confirm a guess?"

"They'll confirm it."

"It's all about reading the signs, isn't it?"

I nod. "Let me go get the cards." I rise from the chair.

"Look!" She points at the window. "The owl is back."

Sure enough, an owl sits on the window ledge, peering at us. "That's a Northern hawk owl. While it's found in Canada and the Upper Peninsula, I've never seen one on the islands here." Her surprised expression has me adding, "I'm a birder, especially of the raptors and owls."

"I'm a birder, too." A pause. "Not many people know that about me. Not even Amanda or Mars. Though I prefer the song birds."

I grin. "Let me go get the cards."

When I return, the owl is still on the ledge, cocking its head one way and then another, its gaze following us in the room.

She says, "You know, this isn't the first owl I've seen." She goes to the chest of drawers, opens one drawer, pulls out a box, and brings it to the table, setting it in front of me.

I run my fingers over the owl engraving.

"I think this box belonged to Margaret's grandfather. I think this owl in the window is somehow connected to him."

"That's astute," I respond.

Quickly I shuffle the cards, and as I shuffle, a card flies out of the deck. I pick it up and turn it over.

Hunter gasps. It's an owl. "What does that mean?"

"In this deck, the owl reveal is a measure of protection."

Pointing at the window, she asks, "Who is this owl protecting?"

"You? Margaret?" I propose.

"We're back to the question of who or what?"

"I can't believe it's Sawyer," I say.

"Aiden!" The loud call comes from someone in the hallway. A workman is calling for me. I gather up the cards and shove them in my pocket. "We'll have to continue this discussion later."

"Thanks for the lessons," she says, as I stride across the room.

At the door, I look her way and smile. "My pleasure."

As I walk down the hall, looking for whoever called me, I'm grateful for the interruption. Hunter is the last person I want analyzing Sawyer. I never should have brought up his name.

Chapter 45

Hunter

Aiden leaves, but my thoughts stay on him and what I've learned. I'm attracted to him and am trying to push my attraction aside. After the house is ready for occupancy, he'll be gone. Oh, we'll bump into each other now and then in Sinclair or elsewhere on the big island, but I doubt that our relationship—

Relationship?! Ha. Who are you kidding?

He isn't interested in me!

With the furniture back in place, there's no reason to stay in my room. I need to busy my hands but more importantly, my mind.

Last night, after reading so much of what Margaret had written about her baby, I'm curious why there was no more reporting on it. The baby was mentioned in the first newspaper report that covered the crime, saying that the baby upstairs in another room had been unharmed. After that one report, nothing was written about the baby, who was taking care of her, or where she had gone.

The ancestor website isn't much help either. Other than the baby being linked to Sawyer and Margaret, there aren't any other family links other than the child she birthed and gave up, with only the birth name, birth date, and death listed. No other relatives. No pictures, no stories, no documents. No history. It's the same for the other adoptees.

So, who inserted these additional adoptees on the website? How did they know about these babies that were given up without there being any other data?

The only reason I became connected was that my DNA was linked to Margaret's DNA and her baby's. Someone somewhere had entered that information. How? And why?

I decide to visit the library and find Lolly, so I can ask what she knows about Margaret and Sawyer's baby.

*****

"All I ever heard were rumors."

Lolly and I are sitting outside behind the library, where they have a picnic table for employees to use while eating packed lunches or taking a break. I found Lolly just at the right time, as she was heading here for a break. This way we're alone, with no one nearby listening.

"What kind of rumors?"

"Oh, the usual. The good, the bad, the nasty." I wait as she pauses and digs into her memory. "I remember one woman—she was vile—saying that no good would ever come of that baby, that it should have been killed, too."

"That *is* nasty."

"Thankfully, she moved away not long after. I think she convinced her husband he needed a different career. She hated Sinclair. Wouldn't surprise me to learn she came back and poisoned the trees."

"There was a problem with poisoned trees back then?"

"Oh, yeah, horrible problem. Some think it was a disgruntled logger who was connected to Frank's bootlegging in some way but couldn't be prosecuted for lack of evidence. Others thought it was her. Turns out they were related somehow." She chuckles.

"Wait a minute. Frank was a bonafide bootlegger?"

"You didn't know that?"

I shake my head. "No, not directly. Is that why she and Frank didn't marry?"

Lolly nods her head.

"There's so much I don't know. Who ended up taking care of the baby?"

"Apparently, Sawyer's stepsister took the baby. And then, once old man Sinclair died after his granddaughter's murder, the connection to the baby was lost. Last I heard back then was that the stepsister had remarried and moved. No one could track her after that."

But, someone had, somewhere along the way, but who? Could it all just be coincidental with lots of people—ancestors of these adoptees—adding to the website's data?

I want to ask Mars.

Chapter 46

Hunter

After docking the boat and entering the house, Daisy greets me. I pick her up and hear Mars' laughter coming from the back of the house. I head to the kitchen to find him. On the way, my stomach growls. I missed lunch and am starving.

If Mars had been in the kitchen, he isn't here any longer. It's empty. I set Daisy down, feed her, and take lunch meat out of the refrigerator. I grab the loaf of bread from the breadbox that sits on the counter next to the refrigerator and spin around, to move toward the island.

A toothpick appears in front of me, at eye-level in the air out of nowhere, and falls to the floor.

Daisy stands in front of me barking, looking up at the area where the toothpick appeared mid-air, her body between my feet as if I'm going to protect her. Her looking up into the air and barking doesn't make sense. The toothpick is on the ground.

My gaze goes from the toothpick up to where Daisy is looking. Is a spirit positioned in front of me? Are they trying to get my attention?

No lilac smell, so it can't be Margaret.

The air temperature hasn't changed either. So, whoever creates the cold spots and cold breezes, it isn't them.

Is this a third ghost?

My little voice says yes. But, who is it?

Toothpicks. Frank used them, but so did Sawyer. Mars, too. Is Mars playing a trick on me?

I look from the spot where the toothpick had appeared and tilt my head back, looking up at the ceiling. I can't see any thread or wire. No hole in the ceiling of any kind, either.

I wave my hand through the space in front of me. Then, I bend over, intending to pick it up.

The door to the outside hall opens. Quickly, I rise without it, staring at the door the whole time.

There's no breeze.

"Amanda?" I ask.

Nothing.

"Mars?"

Nothing.

"Aiden?"

Still nothing.

I take a step toward the open door.

Then stop.

And listen.

Silence.

Almost at the doorway, the hair on the back of my neck stands up, and goosebumps travel up and down my spine and arms. One more step, and I'm in the open doorway. I peer into the unlit hall.

Suddenly, I'm pushed from behind, and the door slams behind me. I scream, missing the three steps as I sail through the air and land on the dirt floor, falling forward onto my knees, first, then my hands. I stop myself from a full-face plant.

Sensing I haven't broken anything, I stand in the blackness, scraping my hands against each other to remove the dirt, then slide my hands along my knees to clean them off.

The door opens behind me.

"Hunter!" Amanda cries. "Are you all right? I was just coming into the kitchen and saw the door slam behind you.

What happened?"

"Oh, not much. Other than being pushed, that is."

Behind Amanda, Mars and Aiden run into the room, coming to a halt behind her. I climb the three steps, and they move, parting, so I can enter the kitchen.

"Are you okay?" they both ask.

"Someone or something pushed me," I repeat.

I don't bother looking at their reactions. I can feel their collective reaction in the silence. I don't care what any of them think at this point. I know I was pushed. By an unseen force that has made its presence known. The hair on the back of my neck rises again.

The three of them follow close behind me until we're standing around the butcher block island where the bread and sandwich meat still sit.

A draft of cold air swirls around us. Aiden looks my way immediately. I nod ever so slightly. Mars and Amanda are arguing with each other, so they miss our exchange.

Now, Aiden is looking at the floor. He notices the toothpick and steps toward it to pick it up.

Mars beats him to it and picks it up himself. "That's mine."

I open my mouth to squelch his claim but see Aiden shake his head just enough for me to notice.

Aiden reaches out for it. "May I?"

Mars frowns, then shrugs his shoulders. He puts it in Aiden's palm.

Aiden brings it to his nostrils and sniffs. "It's been soaked in bourbon."

Frowning, Amanda looks at Mars. "Sawyer used to do that. You never have."

Now it's my turn to frown but at Amanda. "How do you know that about Sawyer?"

She answers, “Mars told me.”

A wisp of air, like a cold fog, appears behind them. They all have their backs to it. The door slams shut.

Amanda jumps, Mars startles, and Aiden turns around.

“It smells like smoke in here,” Amanda says. “I’m beginning to not like this place.” She turns and leaves the room, returning to the main part of the house. Mars follows her.

“What do you think?” Aiden asks.

“I don’t know what to think. Or who to believe. But, I know what I felt minutes ago and what I just saw.”

“What’d you see?”

“A misty form, a spirit, I think. A ghost.”

He nods. “No doubt. The fact that you could see it, either they want you to know they’re here, or your skills are improving. Rapidly. Do you believe me?”

“Yes.” There was no reason to disbelieve him. “Was Frank a smoker?”

“I don’t know. Why?”

“Because the smoke was more like tobacco, not smoke from a fire.”

“We’ll have to check that out. Are you sure you’re okay?”

I nod and open the bread wrapper to finish making my sandwich. “Just going to eat this and then go shopping in the attic for furniture, pictures, and decor.” I want to give my B&B some historic character.

Picking up the finished sandwich, I take a bite and smile at him while chewing. The last thing I want is for him to watch over me while I eat a lousy sandwich.

He leaves, and I plop the sandwich down, swallow, and drink half my water. No, I’m not all right. I was spooked. By spooks.

Up until now, it’s been okay. I’m curious and mystified. But this time, someone was trying to harm me. I know it isn't Margaret. I've had enough encounters with her to know pushing isn't part of her character. It just isn't. Besides, her scent always gives her away. But Sawyer? Given everything that I've read about him in Margaret's diary, I can't believe it's him either. But, I can't tell definitively who it was.

If it isn't Sawyer, who is it? Who pushed me down the stairs? Amanda arrived so quickly after the door slammed, could she have done it and then pretended she just arrived?

I can't believe she would ever hurt me or do something like this, but since arriving here, I've noticed that she's changed. It's almost as if she's mad about something. But, about what? I need to ask her, to be straight with her. We need to do something together so that she'll relax and chat like she normally does. Throughout our friendship, she's generally the one talking. About herself.

I frown. *Wait a minute.* Ever since we arrived here, she hasn't been talking about herself at all.

Why not?

Chapter 47*

Margaret

1922

It's mid-afternoon by the time I return the boat to its hiding place and walk home. As I pass the dock, I see Sawyer tying off his boat. He followed me ashore.

He sees me and heads in my direction, but then he's stopped by another man—a stranger. Sawyer glances my way. He's frowning.

I turn and head home. I arrive and find the household staff in a panic. They're relieved to see me as no one knew where I was. I feel guilty now about taking off like that.

Mary is nowhere to be found.

Grandfather collapsed.

Immediately, I race up to Grandfather's bedroom. He's lying on top of the covers, with an arm over his eyes.

His small davenport-style writing desk is open. He was in the middle of writing a letter. I see the words *bootleggers* and *danger.*

"Sweetheart?"

I turn. He's awake. I step to the bed and take his hand. "What happened?"

He sits up, swinging his legs over the edge of the bed.

"Should you be getting up?"

"I'm fine. I skipped breakfast and then tripped, knocking the wind out of me. Just moved too fast, that's all."

We both turn toward the door, hearing fast footsteps on the

stairs. Sawyer enters the room.

He frowns, seeing me there. "May I talk with your grandfather, please? Alone?"

Grandfather tugs on my hand, pats it, and says, "It's okay. I need to talk with him."

I close the door behind me and start downstairs, but not before I hear Sawyer say, "Tell me everything that happened."

Downstairs, the cook asks me about dinner. I tell her to prepare as usual. I don't know who will be here or when, but we have to eat, so it might as well be ready.

I go out the front door and take a step to the side and lean against the wall, letting the screen door shut, and take a deep breath.

Unable to stand here like this, just waiting for Sawyer to come down, I go into the yard and around the house to the backyard where laundry needs to be removed from the line.

Half done with the chore, I'm reaching for a sheet when I hear, "Mary—" and then there's a hand on my hip.

I turn. It's Frank.

He's surprised to see me but recovers quickly. He laughs and gives me a tight hug. "I knew it was you. Don't know why I said the wrong name." Then, he pulls back and looks down at the ground. "Is your grandfather around?"

"Inside."

Without another word, he kisses my cheek, turns, and walks around the house in search of Grandfather.

I stand there, my head spinning. Instinct tells me he didn't just say the wrong name. He's never put a hand on my hip like that. Ever. And, he knows Grandfather's habits well. Why would he look for Grandfather in the backyard when he should have gone directly inside first?

I debate whether to skip the laundry and follow him inside,

but storm clouds growing darker overhead with the wind picking up warn me to finish the chore first.

Chapter 48

Hunter

Present Day

I sit in the rocking chair, watching the night sky. The view through my bedroom windows of the moon, the planets, and stars is incredible.

Today was another long day.

It feels like I've lived here for weeks and weeks, but it's only been a week. How is that even possible?

The transformation of the multiple bathrooms is remarkable. The team Aiden hired is fast. It was nearly dark by the time we sat down for dinner. Aiden says they'll be finished with the bathrooms tomorrow or the day after, at which time, they'll be ripping out the kitchen.

When I commented at dinner that I'll have to pack up the kitchen, Amanda offered to do it, which is fine by me. I'm tired of packing and unpacking, which reminds me that I need to communicate with my Detroit realtor tomorrow to see if there were any problems when she did a walk-through of Mom and Dad's house—my other house. Since I haven't heard from her, I suspect everything's okay, that she listed the house as we talked about before I came north, but even so, I still want to check in with her.

Tomorrow, Amanda will be in the kitchen, and Mars and Aiden will be helping the team finish the bathrooms. I'm going to do general cleanup after everyone, plus snoop around in the attic.

When dinner is done and Aiden and I are the last to leave the table, I pick up Aiden's and my plates and silverware and put my fingers into our empty glasses to carry them into the kitchen.

Aiden pushes back his chair and stands. "Thanks." He slides a hand into his pocket, pulls it out, and slides a toothpick into the side of his mouth.

I stare at him.

These toothpicks are messing with my mind.

Earlier, after Mars had picked up the toothpick from the kitchen floor, Aiden claimed it was his. I knew it didn't belong to either of them. It had appeared in mid-air, right in front of me. Had Aiden always used toothpicks like Mars? Like Sawyer and Frank?

I never knew Mars to soak his toothpicks in bourbon, but Sawyer had. Mars doesn't like bourbon. Was Sawyer the ghost I'd seen in the kitchen? Could he have been the one to push me?

No. Sawyer pushing me doesn't feel right. How can I straighten out these multiple toothpick events? It's so confusing!

Rising from the chair, I go to the window and close it a bit against the cooler evening air. Soon, it'll be too cold to leave the windows open at night. Instead, I leave it open a crack, so I can wake up, hearing the birds singing.

In bed, despite feeling tired, I pick up Margaret's diary. It's become a habit to read some pages before turning off the light.

Sawyer created a secret door. I watched him install it and couldn't believe how it disappeared completely when he shut it. Anyone could be standing right next to it and not see it.

Was she talking about the attic door? How many times had I stood next to it and not seen it?

After all that nasty bootlegging business, I don't ever want to see that room again. I don't want anyone to know it's there. The government came and took away the barrels after Frank went to jail.

That's *why* he went to jail? For bootlegging? Is that why she and Frank broke up? Because she found out he was involved in criminal behavior?

Sawyer said he'd provide camouflage in front of the secret door, for my peace of mind. Our peace of mind. He didn't care to use the room for anything else—ever—and wanted us to forget it was there.

Puzzled, I stash the diary back in its box. Call me paranoid. I don't want Mars or Amanda to see the duplicate box and discover there's another diary. For some unknown reason, I want to keep it hidden from the others. I'm not sure why, but I feel the need to keep it a secret for now.

I'm learning to follow my gut instincts even if I don't know the reason why I should each time. I lay the box on the side table, and will put it back into its hiding space in the morning since I can't do it now from this higher level. Something I can't do while in bed.

The worst thing about it all is that Amanda and Mars have been my best friends for most of my life. How can I not trust them?

I scooch down under the sheet, pull it up to my neck, and smooth the sheet on either side of my body, lying perfectly still on my back. With the room dark and the curtains open, I have a wonderful view of the night sky.

An owl hoots.

Lilacs.

I expect the chair to start rocking, but it doesn't even though I sense that she's here now.

Goosebumps rise on my arms and down my legs. My indicator that my senses are spot on.

My sensitivity to the unseen has grown immensely. Is it

because of the ghosts? The history of this house? Would my ability to detect ghosts have evolved like this had I stayed in Detroit?

I don't think so. At least, not as quickly as I've been experiencing it all these last few days.

It must be the house. Because I'm connected to it? Actually, I *am* tied to this house. By blood. Deeply connected. Margaret is family.

And, the secret door she wrote about—wait a minute. She isn't talking about the attic door. The attic wasn't locked up for good or camouflaged so no one could enter it. Camouflaged, yes. But, not to keep people from entering it. From what I have seen in the attic, some of the furniture is from before the turn of the last century, which means *her* grandfather put it there. How much was stored up there after Margaret's death? Hard to tell. At any rate, the attic is too ordinary a room. It isn't hidden, nor is it a secret.

So, if it isn't the attic and its door, where is this secret room? There isn't one up here on the second floor. Nor, on the first floor. Not that I know of, but do I know that for sure? How can I find out?

I could measure the rooms from the inside and then measure the house on the outside. Wouldn't all the rooms have to fit within those measurements? If the outside measure is bigger than the inside, then wouldn't that indicate a secret space? How can I find out without a tape measure?

I decide to rise early to pace off the rooms and do the same outside.

Hopefully, no one will see me. It'll just be easier that way with no one questioning me.

I go to sleep with a plan.

Chapter 49

Hunter

It's been two days of decisions, people coming and going, and my being a runner for Aiden and his crew. The bathrooms are nearly finished. Today, Mars is putting up all the knobs and racks, attending to all the little details. He enjoys shiny things.

Aiden's men tore out the kitchen yesterday. Stripped it down to nothing, then sanded the wooden floors.

Now, Aiden, Mars, and Aiden's crew are bringing in new appliances and cabinets through the back door. A more direct route for sure. Initially, I was in the way, so I'm standing behind the kitchen's open door. All the men are here except for Mars. Did he get stuck somewhere?

I peer around the door and peek into the hallway.

The woodpile that had been stacked along one of the walls was removed, giving the men more room. With doors open at both ends and a couple of lanterns hanging from the ceiling, light fills the hallway.

Mars has a drawer under his arm and another hanging from his left hand. He stopped in the middle of the hallway and is now sliding his right hand along the wall where the wood had been stacked.

At one point, he jerks, turns his head toward his hand, and moves closer, peering, and rubbing his hand over one spot. Out of the corner of his eye, he sees me and quickly drops his hand, grinning. "You know me and textures. Especially wood grains."

He comes into the kitchen, handing over the drawers, which

get slid into the cabinets. And then, they all go back outside to get more cabinets and supplies.

As they disappear out of sight, I step down into the hallway and over to the spot Mars had been inspecting.

I don't see anything different. What did he see that interested him so much?

I run my hand along the wall like he did.

I feel something.

A whiff of air.

I drop my hand and look around. With both hall doors open, air is flowing through the hall. But, what had he felt? Would he have remained inspecting it more closely had he not been surprised at seeing me there?

I lean over so I can look at that spot more closely.

I see nothing.

I straighten and frown at the wall. Could this be the hidden room Margaret had written about in her diary?

If there is a room behind the hallway, hopefully, I can find it before he does.

Now that I think about it, there very well could be a room there. My goal of measuring the house inside and out was only partially achieved before I got interrupted by the arrival of the men. As I consider the dimensions at the back of the house, here, the outside wall at the back of the house is flat. So, what's between the outside wall and the kitchen wall? It must be a storeroom of some kind.

Wait a minute. Margaret talked about barrels being removed. Were they from Frank's bootlegging operation? Kept in a storage room? Now a hidden room?

Hearing the men returning, I scurry up the stairs and out of the kitchen. I don't want Mars or anyone else to see me hovering at the wall.

I need to watch Mars more carefully.

Chapter 50*

Margaret

1922

With the laundry basket under my arm, I barely get inside ahead of the rain. Five minutes later, I'm finally able to check in with Grandfather. Right away, he says, "Something isn't adding up."

"How so?"

"Did Frank come out and talk with you at all?"

"Not really. At first, he thought I was Mary. Once he corrected himself, he came to see you right away."

He has that thoughtful look that tells me he's analyzing, pondering.

"What aren't you telling me?"

"Mary—what do you really know about her?"

What a strange question! "We've been best friends for a decade. I've learned a lot from her."

He nods, then says more to himself than to me, "It was his comment about her and Sawyer—"

"You mean Theodore."

"No, Frank was specific about Sawyer and her returning to Detroit together."

"But Theodore's from New York," I inject.

Grandfather nods. "Do you know where Sawyer is?"

"Working on the house, I assume. Didn't he go back to the island after talking with you?

"You need to get a message to him." Grandfather scribbles

on a piece of paper, then folds it and puts it in a sealed envelope, not writing anything on the outside. He holds it up to me.

I took it and put it in my pants pocket.

"Don't let anyone see you going to the island."

"You want me to take our secret fishing boat?"

He nods. "Row to the side of the island. There's a secret inlet, just like the one here in Sinclair where we keep our hidden row boat. Don't let anyone see you walk up to the house."

I laugh. "You make it sound like there's multiple people on Harbor House Island. Sawyer's the only one there."

"Just be careful. And, hurry."

I don't like that he's being vague, nor do I want to leave him in this agitated state, but he needs my help, so I leave. The rain starts as I step off the porch. I'm glad I grabbed by raincoat, a long dark gray wrap with a hood. My thoughts are spinning. The entire time I rush to the boat—but then slow to a stroll anytime someone is looking—and row to the island. What's going on?

Why was Frank looking for Mary?

Why did Grandfather imply that Mary is connected to Sawyer?

And, who could hurt me?

Thankfully, because of the pouring rain, I'm shielded from view once I row away from Sinclair. If I can't see the docks or shoreline, then I won't be seen either.

Who does Grandfather want to hide me from? Why can't I be going for a normal visit?

But then, this isn't a normal visit, is it? The trip is wrapped in secrecy and feels like an undercover reconnaissance. With Sawyer. Does this have anything to do with the increase of boats I've seen on the lake lately and the sudden influx of strangers on Drummond Island? Granted, we get loggers looking for work frequently, but these men aren't loggers, not the way they're dressed and come through the village as if on a mission.

As I approach the island, I see three boats docked. Then, a pounding rain obscures my view of the docks. They've become invisible, just as I have. Good.

As I slide into the secret slip, the rain stops though it's still gray and dark. I take off the raincoat and leave it in the boat.

From this vantage point, I can see both the front dock and part of the back beach.

That's when I see Sawyer on the beach with a lantern, waving it back and forth. Suddenly, a light appears on the lake halfway between us and Canada. A boat with a couple men standing in the boat's bow, and they're wearing black. Raincoats most likely—then I see a sudden flash of red that's quickly covered. Another lantern?

Is Sawyer a bootlegger? No, he can't be, not with Grandfather sending me after him, but what if Grandfather doesn't know Sawyer's true identity?

Sawyer turns and enters the house through the back. I decide to follow him rather than expose my presence by going through the front door.

I squat down to stay hidden amongst the shrubbery. I hug the stone wall, sliding along the house until I can slip through the back door that is open. I peer to ensure the hallway is empty first. I don't want to appear as a shadow, surprising someone.

Behind me, I can see that the Canadian boat is heading straight to this island.

Quickly, I enter the house, go through the kitchen, then climb the few stairs to the dining room, hesitating and listening as I move quietly. About to enter the room, I'm grabbed from behind, a hand covering my mouth, silencing my scream, pulling me back down into the kitchen, lifting me so my feet no longer touch the ground.

Chapter 51*

Margaret

I struggle against my captor.

"Stop fighting me."

Sawyer's voice. I stop. As he's talking, he turns me around and sets me down, his hands around my upper arms preventing me from moving anywhere. "You're in danger, Meggie. Nothing is as it seems."

I gasp. Sawyer *IS* Johnny!

I reach into my pocket and hand him Grandfather's message.

He rips it open, reads it quickly, then thrusts it into his pocket.

"We've got to get you out of here. Fast!"

We hear movement from another part of the house, but then it stops. He hands me a gun. I shake my head and try to hand it back.

"Just in case. Leave in the boat the way you came. The Mounties are coming. We've set a trap, and I can't lose you again."

He turns me around and pushes me gently toward the hall door and into the hall.

"Hurry," he says, then disappears.

I'm outside, hugging the stone wall again, then step into the shrubbery, and am hidden within it when a noise from the front corner of the house alerts me that someone is coming.

I freeze.

Chapter 52

Mars

Present Day

At the end of the day, the four of us sit around the dining room table, enjoying the lasagna and salad Amanda brought back from Sinclair since we can't use the kitchen to cook. We thought she was going after pizza, but she fooled us.

There's still a lot to do in the kitchen, but at least we have a functional sink and countertop. Cabinets are up but lack hardware and doors. They'll go on tomorrow. A new refrigerator and stove are being delivered tomorrow, too.

"The kitchen will be finished by the end of tomorrow," Aiden says.

"I can't wait for it to be a fully functional kitchen," Hunter says.

"I'll help you get it set up," Amanda offers.

"Deal!" Hunter exclaims. "How is it that work always goes faster when there are two of us?"

Amanda continues. "At least if you do decide to sell, everything will be up to code and modernized."

Purposefully, I shift the conversation. "The men were talking about Sawyer today. What do you think happened to him?" I ask. "Strange that he was never found. Either dead or alive."

"Just as strange that Frank was never found either," Amanda says. "From what I've learned, he and Margaret were quite the power couple until he screwed up."

"And cheating on Margaret the entire time," Aiden says.

I have information about Frank from earlier research, but I'm not ready to reveal it yet. Would I ever tell? I don't know. It's not like Hunter or Amanda is related to him.

I ask, "Do you think either one of them killed the other?"

Aiden replies. "Anything's possible."

Amanda pushes back her chair and collects my empty plate with hers. "I'll wash if you dry."

I'd rather not, but I say, "Sure," and collect dirty dishes and follow her into the kitchen.

Chapter 53

Hunter

After dinner, and after Amanda and Mars are done with the dishes, Aiden calls us upstairs. I know what's going on, but Amanda and Mars don't. Aiden and I decided earlier, it would be better this way because if they knew, they'd freak out and refuse to participate. Especially Amanda. Once she gets something in her head, there's no changing her mind.

I lead Mars and Amanda into my bedroom where Aiden is already there, waiting for us.

Inside the room, Mars and Amanda see a card table and chairs in the middle of the room.

"What's this?" Amanda asks.

Aiden steps to her and guides her to a chair. "Have a seat."

Automatically, I sit opposite her. Mars and Aiden sit in the chairs opposite each other. Boy, girl, boy, girl.

Instantly, Amanda is suspicious. Her gaze darts around to all of us. "Did you know about this?" she asks Mars.

"What are we doing?" Mars asks. "Playing hearts?"

Aiden sticks a short, squatty candle on a plate in the middle of the table.

Amanda eyes the candle, me, and then Aiden. "What's the candle for?"

"We're calling the spirits," I announce, "and you're both going to participate. For me."

Amanda glares. She knows that I know how much she doesn't want to be doing this. For all the times she made me do something I didn't want to do, this is now payback time. And, she knows it. The way her jaw clenches, she's grinding her teeth.

Like Amanda, Mars looks at us with suspicion, but he appears to be okay with going along with it. He doesn't believe any of this hoodoo voodoo, as he calls it, but I know he's curious.

Aiden no sooner lights the candle and shows us how to hold our hands on the table, palm up, with one of our hands laying in the palm of another when the curtains billow out broadly and lilacs scent the air.

Without thinking, I ask, "Is that you, Margaret?"

The candle flickers, and a soft breeze swirls around us. It's as if the scent is rising, floating toward the ceiling.

Then suddenly, a bold, warm breeze circles us in the opposite direction and plasters the filmy, lightweight curtains against the windows.

"There's two spirits here," Aiden says.

I say, "Margaret and—"

"Something evil!" Amanda gushes. Her hand is beneath mine, and her fingers curl around my hand, gripping me tightly. Mars cringes. She's doing the same thing to him with her other hand.

He pulls his hand out of hers and shakes it. "Easy, there, Mandy."

His use of his nickname for her relaxes her a bit. Just a tiny bit.

"Can these spirits hurt us?" she asks Aiden.

"No. If they try, just tell them to stop."

"But—"

"Amanda," he says. "You're in charge. They can pick up on your fear and they'll play on it if you let them."

"It's that simple?"

He nods. "The movies and ghost hunter programs want you

to think otherwise."

She let go of our hands and sits back. "Who is it? Are you friendly?"

The curtains drift out into the room again, and the scent of lilacs returns.

I say, "I think Margaret is telling us that whoever it is, they're protecting her."

"And us," Aiden adds.

"Sawyer?" Amanda asks.

Aiden nods his head. "That'd be my guess."

"But not Frank?" Mars asks.

"Do you think Frank came back here?" I ask Mars.

Mars lifts one shoulder in a questioning shrug. "Why not?"

"What would he be looking for?" Aiden asks, his expression pointed and directed at Mars.

I frown. Aiden's tone isn't one of curiosity. What does Aiden know that he isn't telling me? His focus on Mars is almost accusatory.

Amanda stands quickly. "Are we done?"

My frustration with Amanda is growing by the day. It's almost as if she doesn't want to be here, and yet, she was so enthusiastic in the beginning.

She looks at Mars. "You coming?"

Mars glances at me and Aiden, then back at me again. I'm not giving him anything.

He appears puzzled that I'm not saying anything. "Yeah, I'm coming."

He gets up, and the two of them leave with me and Aiden still sitting at the table.

"What was that about?" I ask.

"I'm not sure, but I have the feeling that they both know something they're not telling."

“I agree but what is it you think they know? Think they’re in it together?” I don’t know why I asked the second question, but somehow I don’t think they are despite their history. While growing up, they were always conspiring with each other, hatching one plan or another where I would learn about it after the fact. This time, something feels different. He looks at me sharply. “What are you suspecting?”

“I don’t know. Just listening to my feelings, I guess.”

He nods and then grins. “Good girl.”

“Do you think the second spirit is Frank?”

“At first, I thought so, feeling like the second spirit was chasing Margaret away, but when she returned, it was almost as if she was embracing the second spirit. It wasn’t cold, just forceful.”

“You think it’s Sawyer then?”

“It could be anyone, at this point. Another clue sure would be helpful.”

Aiden rises and just as I rise, it happens again. I freeze. A toothpick appears out of thin air just behind Aiden and drops to his side.

He turns and sees me staring at the ground.

“What?” he asks.

I point to the toothpick on the floor. “It appeared out of thin air. Like before.”

“In the kitchen?”

I nod. “The toothpick that Mars says was his and which you claimed was yours instead.”

Aiden bends over and picks it up. He sniffs it. “Bourbon.”

“Sawyer.”

Aiden nods. “Unless you think Mars left it.”

I shake my head. “I’m telling you. I saw it appear out of nowhere, right beside you, in the air.”

He doesn’t say anything.

I ask, "You believe me, don't you?"
"With everything I've seen, why would I doubt you?"

Chapter 54*

Margaret

1922

Mary and Frank, holding hands, come around the corner and stop about twenty-five feet from me, oblivious to my presence.

They hug, laugh, and kiss briefly. Then Frank says, "We made it out. No one's the wiser. All we have to do is get onboard the boat coming from Canada. This way." Together, they continue stepping toward the back of the house.

I step out of the bushes and point the gun at them. Instantly, they drop their handhold.

They're stunned seeing me there.

"We're looking for Sawyer," Mary says.

"Sawyer!" I yell.

Frank laughs. "You're such a fool. He's with us."

"And, you're the bigger fool," I say. "He's not." Mary gasps, and Frank looks surprised. I yell again for Sawyer.

Frank's face is ugly as he charges toward me.

I shoot.

He goes down, grabbing his leg.

Stunned, Mary looks at Frank on the ground. She snarls and rushes at me. I sidestep at the right moment and trip her. She falls to the ground.

I run around to the front, climb the steps quickly, and start ringing the bell.

Suddenly, men come out of bushes where I'd left my boat. I

point them to where I'd left Mary and Frank.

Sawyer runs out of the front door and stops.

Instantly, another time when we stood like this comes to mind. He has those same brown eyes, a look that pierces my soul now, just as it did back then.

"You're safe."

I nod.

"Looks like you've learned how to take better care of yourself."

I nod again and slowly grin.

And then, I hear the words I uttered that day. "Marry me."

I wrap my arms around his neck and pull him down, and breathe, "Yes!" and kiss him just like our first kiss had been like, only longer this time.

Reluctant to stop but breathless, I pull back just a little.

His breath warm on my face, his gaze locked on my lips and eyes dark with desire, he says, "I've been wanting to do that ever since I first saw you boarding the steamer in Detroit."

"You had a stateroom and hid in it, didn't you?"

He nods. "I didn't trust myself around you."

Chapter 55

Hunter

Present Day

I spend the next day doing odd tasks, mending a few curtain hems, and touching up scratches and dings over the years, vacuuming furniture, crevices and corners, and the stairs. Wanting to keep busy and not think about what happened last night.

Aiden and I talked for a short bit after the toothpick appeared, but we didn't come to any resolutions. It's all so puzzling, and he's just as puzzled as I am.

I'm cleaning and polishing the dining room table when Danny comes out of the kitchen telling me that their work is finished. The kitchen is done just in time for dinner.

They leave, announcing they'll return tomorrow to work on the outside of the house.

Eager to see the finished room, I enter the kitchen and admire the work. A gleaming stainless-steel refrigerator captures my attention, and then the six-burner gas stove. I'm ecstatic at the size and scope of where a cook can prepare meals for my future guests. The small table and small island have been replaced with an enormous island that accommodates bar stools. The workers even provided a cubby at the end of the island for Daisy's dishes, so they're out of the way of anyone tripping over them.

That's when I see her dishes are still full of food. She hasn't eaten all day. I frown. Now that I think about it, I haven't seen her all day.

I call out to her.

Silence.

No answering bark or hearing her nails on the wooden floor.

I go into the main part of the house, calling her.

Nothing.

Amanda is coming downstairs. "What's wrong?"

I haven't seen Amanda all day either. Has she been avoiding me because of last night?

"I can't find Daisy. Have you seen her?"

"Is she lost?"

"I don't know. Have you seen her upstairs?" I ask. I start climbing the stairs. I'll search every room until I find her. Hopefully, she hasn't eaten anything she shouldn't have. "Come help me look."

Amanda follows me upstairs, and we go down one hall together, each of us taking a bedroom on either side of the hall. I hear her calling for Daisy just as I am. I hear doors opening and closing, too. Likewise, I check the closets and bathrooms. Any space she could have gotten into. And, of course, under the bed.

Room by room, Amanda and I check until we reach the end of the hall.

We return to the stairway and begin searching the rooms down the opposite hall. If she isn't in any of these rooms, there's only one more hallway to cover; bedrooms that aren't being used.

By the time we finish searching through the second hallway's rooms, Mars is coming up the stairs. He went to town earlier and must have just returned. "I heard the commotion," he says, meeting us on the landing. "You looking for Daisy?"

"She's missing," Amanda says.

"Has been all day, I think," I add. "Her food hasn't been touched.

"I was downstairs in the kitchen," he says, "In that little

closet off the kitchen."

"The pantry?" I ask.

"Yeah. I was putting away some groceries—"

"Don't tell me," Amanda snarks. "Another hidden door?"

Mars snarls and actually growls at her.

"Sorry," she mumbles.

"And?" I question.

"When I opened the door, I heard her growling.

"What?" both Amanda and I exclaim.

"How?" I ask.

"There's a vent in the ceiling," Aiden says from behind us. "All the rooms have those vents."

We turn in unison as he joins our huddle. "Back before central heating, it was a way for the heat to rise naturally upstairs and into the rooms directly. I heard what you were saying as I came up the stairs." He asks Mars, "What room were you in, did you say?"

"The pantry off the kitchen."

Aiden points to the third hallway and the rooms that are situated over the back of the house. "Then Daisy must be down here somewhere."

We all move in that direction.

"You girls take these front rooms, and Mars and I will take the back ones," Aiden directs us.

We follow his directions.

I've barely started my search when I hear Aiden exclaim, "Here she is!"

Back in the hall, we gather around Aiden with Daisy wiggling in his arms, licking him. He hands her to me, and she excitedly licks me.

"Mystery solved," Amanda says.

"I guess that means we all go back to work," Mars adds.

The two of them leave. I wait until they're out of earshot and turn to Aiden. "Where was she? Why couldn't we hear her when we were up here?

"She was in the bathroom and there was a towel covering the gap under the door. Probably to muffle any sound."

"Why pick on Daisy? What has she done?"

"I don't think it was about Daisy. I think it was about you."

"Me? What have I done? Who do you suspect?" I ask.

"I'm not sure anymore."

"Could a ghost have done it?"

"And put a towel under the door?" he asks.

"Why not? Stranger things have been going on. Like the toothpicks."

"True, but this smells more like human intervention rather than from a spirit." He frowns and puts a hand on my arm. Immediately, the warmth comforts me. "You don't suspect me, do you?"

"No, of course not," I say in a rush. No, I don't suspect him, but at the same time, how well do I know him? Yes, I'm attracted to him, but I have no clue how he feels about me.

Can I fully trust him? So far, he hasn't said or done anything to make me distrust him. Not yet anyway.

Chapter 56

Aiden

The minute I was introduced to Hunter, I was smitten. It took everything I had not to ask her out on a date the first minute we were alone.

I want her in my life, but I know if I'm not careful I could scare her away.

So, I'm taking my time. Leading. Somewhat. Guiding. Letting her come to her own conclusions, which have no doubt created questions.

During our two séances, I watched her confidence grow. She's more attuned to the spirits in this house than I am. Her senses are stronger than she realizes. I love this about her—that she wants to learn and grow. And, investigate without fear.

The problem, though, is I've kept something from her. I sense she doesn't tolerate lying; yet, at the same time, I think she's been hiding a secret or two of her own.

She has no idea how she's pursuing these spirits with courage, as if she's unafraid. Her curiosity far outweighs any fear.

I want to be careful in how I proceed from here. It takes time to build trust but only a second to destroy it?

Chapter 57

Hunter

Later, I find Amanda, and we talk, reconciling as we always have in the past.

Now, we're going through the house, headed for the back door to look for sea glass on the Canadian side beach. A cold front came through, bringing angry waves. Amanda is wearing my hoodie with the hood up, while I'm in layers.

She opens the hall door in the kitchen, and I stop to refill my water bottle. She waits for me by the door.

My water bottle filled, I turn and am almost to her when I see a mist forming behind her.

Amanda arches her back unnaturally and falls down the stairs.

She was pushed!

Someone pushed her lower back, causing her back to arch like that.

Just as I had been.

I stand there, stunned, staring. The mist floats down into the hallway. At the doorway, I watch it move through and past Amanda. I go to her and help her up. The opaque form hovers in the middle of the hallway as if to block us.

Amanda screams.

"Go away!" I shout and rush toward it. No spirit from the other side is going to threaten me.

I stop a step too late. Cold covers me. I'm in the mist. And then, it moves off me and disappears through the wall.

Through the secret door.

Now, I'm more curious than ever and, surprisingly, not frightened a bit.

I told it to leave, and it did. Aiden was right—I hold all the power. I'm the one in control. These ghosts are here as my guests. They're invading *my* home. It isn't theirs any longer to haunt. Not if they're going to harm me. Margaret can stay, but this one has to go.

The familiar goosebumps I've come to recognize when acknowledging a truth travel up and down my arms and spine.

"I can't believe you just did that," Amanda says from behind me.

I turn around. "Are you okay?" I ask.

"Just shaken up. What was that?"

"A ghost."

"No way." She shakes her head. "This is too much. I can't deal with this, no matter what Mars says."

"What do you mean, *what Mars says?*"

"You have no idea, do you? He's known about your family for a long time. For some reason, he wanted access to this place. I'm leaving. I can't do this any longer."

She runs up the few steps into the kitchen and disappears into the dining room. I stand there listening to her steps fading, grappling at her revelation of Mars' actions. Now, she's running up the stairs. To pack, I presume.

I turn to the wall and stare. I raise my left hand and place it on the wall. The wall Mars had been inspecting the other day.

Mars. My so-called best friend.

How long has he been playing me? And Amanda?

It appears they both have.

If she leaves like this, she'll never return. Is this going to be the end of our relationship?

Has Mars been looking for the secret door the entire time we've been here? The one Margaret wrote about in her diary? If this secret door *is* the one Sawyer and Margaret closed, then who is hanging around it like this?

Does this hidden door Margaret wrote about have something to do with Frank's bootlegging activity? The real reason he wanted to marry Margaret?

I move my hand around the wall.

How did Mars know about the door?

Because of her diaries, only Margaret, Sawyer, and I know the door was made secret. But how many others knew of the rear entrance back then? Anyone involved with the bootlegging and then the removal of the barrels—but those people are long gone. Dead.

What about Aiden? What does he know about it? I never did follow up about his knowledge of old houses. Would he have ever seen a floor plan of this house?

None of this explains how Mars would know.

Daisy joins me. I bend to pet her. She sniffs at the ground and wall, then starts pawing the ground at the wall. I push her away and put my hand where her paw was. She sniffs around my hand.

A wisp of air moves. The outer door hasn't been opened yet. So, how am I feeling air coming out of the wall? If that's a room on the other side of this door, there's no window. I've checked the outside perimeter. So, if there aren't any windows, how can air be moving?

I move my hand upward, following the air. It's nothing more than a slight tickle on my palm. I lean forward and sniff.

I jerk back, gagging and coughing. It smells musty and old. And something else. Are there dead rodents in there?

This has to be the room that Margaret was talking about in

her diary. The room Sawyer sealed.

I go in search of Aiden. I need some help if I'm going to open it. But, I want to ask a few questions before I bring him down here.

First, though, I need to talk to Amanda.

Chapter 58

Amanda

Up in my room, I tear off the hoodie and throw it on the floor. That's the last time I'll ever borrow anything of Hunter's again!

No doubt that ghost thought I was her! Horrified at what just happened, I don't even want it in my room!

I pick up the hoodie and go to Hunter's room. I know she isn't in there, so I open the door and place the garment on her bed.

The handmade wooden box she opened at the restaurant back home on her birthday sits on the tabletop next to the bed. But, wait a minute. It isn't the same box. It's slightly different. Same coloring, same shape, but the lid icon is different.

I pick it up. It has an owl carved on the cover. I open it. A book—no, it's a diary inside.

Is this where she's been getting her information? What hasn't she been telling us?

"What are you doing?!?"

I jump, startled by Hunter's voice. The box flies out of my hands.

Both of us try to grab it. Instead, it crashes onto the rug beside the bed.

CRACK!

It breaks, and a picture falls out of it along with the diary.

Hunter bends and picks up the photo. I peer at it over her shoulder. I recognize Margaret's grandfather, but who is the other guy? Hunter flips the photo over.

It's blank. She turns it right side up again and lays the picture on the table, picking up the box, examining the pieces. In an instant, she puts the pieces together, places the picture in the drawer, and then slides the drawer back into the box. I wouldn't have known the drawer existed had I not seen Hunter close it just now. When closed, the drawer melds into the box perfectly. Appearing nonexistent.

It's the drawer that broke away from the box. Otherwise, the box is unharmed. And, the drawer appears to be part of the bottom of the box.

"Why was the picture hidden in the box?"

"I don't know," Hunter replies.

"Whose box is it?"

Hunter looks at the front cover again, fingering the owl carving. "I don't know that either," she says, "but I'm wondering if it belonged to Sawyer." Her voice drops as if she's talking to herself. "If it is, why hide the picture?"

She picks up the picture from the table and studies it again.

Watching her, I want to help her find answers, but deep in my heart, I know I can't. This place is haunted. For real.

Seeing actual ghosts is scary!

What was Mars thinking that we could deceive Hunter? She's determined to find answers. If there is any treasure to be found in this house, it belongs to Hunter, not Mars.

He's idiotic thinking there's buried treasure in a secret room and that it belongs to him. I'm a fool for going along with his crazy scheme. Stupidly, I believed him when he said he'd divide it between us. I was driven by greed and wanted to work closely with him.

I'm ready to go home. There's no way Hunter is ever going to leave this place. She's in love with it. The house, the island, and with Aiden, too, even if she doesn't realize it.

A mower starts up, and we both turn toward the open window.

Hunter puts the box down. With the picture in hand, she steps to the window.

I follow her.

Aiden is mowing what little bit of lawn that is between the house and the dock about fifty yards away. With all the vegetation that grows wild around the house, there isn't much lawn to maintain.

Hunter pushes away from the window. "I'm going to get some answers. Don't leave yet. I'll protect you. We'll talk later."

I'm sure we will. I'm curious about things, too, but unlike Hunter, I'm willing to walk away from them all.

I need a break from these loony people. I'll be happy if I never see or hear of a ghost ever again.

Chapter 59

Hunter

Aiden looks up and turns off the mower as I descend the front steps and approach him.

"What's up?" he asks.

I thrust the picture at him. "I recognize the guy on the right as Margaret's grandfather. Who's he with?"

Aiden looks at the picture and then at me with what I can only describe as an instant of not wanting to answer. He looks back down at the picture again. "Where did you get this?"

"In a secret drawer in a box that I found in Margaret's room. The box was hidden in the nightstand's bottom drawer." I frown. I venture a guess. "You know who this is, don't you?"

His lips round as if he's going to say no, but then he stops. Instead, he says, "Yes, I do."

I need to see his reaction to what else I know. "I saw that man in another picture. One you have in your collection upstairs. I remember you telling me he was your great-great-grandfather."

He hands me the photograph. "Yes."

"And, he's with George Sinclair, Margaret's grandfather because...?"

"He's Sawyer's father."

I stare at him. Whatever I thought his answer might be, it sure wasn't this. "You're related to Sawyer? He's your great-grandfather?"

"Yes. Sawyer's father was here asking Sinclair if he'd hire Johnny for the summer. He wanted Johnny out of the city because he was getting involved with gangs."

"Johnny?"

"Jonathan Sawyer Van Houten. He dropped his first name shortly after returning home."

"The Johnny Margaret had proposed to when she was six?"

"The same." Aiden grins. "Sawyer told the family about the story when he came home, after he'd been fired, how he had defended Meggie against bullies and defended her father against some mobsters by not revealing the truth to Meggie's grandfather. That's what he always called her at home—Meggie. George Sinclair had no idea there were mobsters in his company of loggers. It's the main reason Sawyer became a lawman. He hated bullies. He was able to work and return undercover on Drummond Island because no one recognized him. He only revealed his identity to the elder Sinclair."

"So how did he end up missing, thought to have killed his wife?"

"That's the mystery I've been wanting to solve. But, I needed access to the island. I was hoping I could find secrets here that haven't been revealed so far. The family knew Johnny as a kind, gentle boy. That's what both Meggie and her grandfather had seen, too. Meggie's father, Edward, was a gambler and was being blackmailed to do the mob's bidding. As a boy, Johnny put himself between a rock and a hard wall of resistance when dealing with Sinclair in trying to protect her father."

"Did Sinclair know this?"

Aiden nods. "He strongly suspected, but Sinclair could never prove anything, and his son wasn't saying. By keeping his mouth shut, Johnny got himself fired. Three proud men, even if one of them was just a boy of thirteen at the time." Aiden takes a deep breath and lets it out with a sigh. "I'm sorry that I wasn't totally honest with you in the beginning. I wasn't sure what you knew or how you came to know it. I had to be able to trust you completely."

I look out across the dock to Sinclair in the distance. He's had the same trust issues I've had but for different reasons. Does he still? "It's been a puzzle for sure. If only—"

A breeze from the south stirs the bushes and treetops. A moan sounds. I turn and look at the lilac bushes.

A mist without form appears out of nowhere at the bottom of the stairs and drifts across the lawn. Into the lilac bushes.

And disappears.

I step in that direction, unable to stop staring at the bushes, with Aiden beside me.

We both stop at the edge of the bushes. I move around toward the back where I find a bit of a path in. How can that be? I missed it because I was never on this side of the lilacs.

I step into the slight break in the branches. A tiny way in. I duck and take a few steps. Suddenly, I'm clear of the branches that grow outward and can stand upright. It's as if I'm in a secret hideout.

An enormous pile of leaves is layered across most of this clearing. Leaves from the bushes. They've been here for decades. Untouched. The clearing is about the length of my body. I could easily lie down and not touch any of the trunks or branches.

Aiden grabs my arm to stop me from moving forward.

He's staring at the ground in front of us.

I gasp.

A bone. A white spot on an otherwise brown landscape. A couple inches of a smooth, curved bone is exposed. A skull? Aiden bends and brushes away a few leaves.

Most definitely a skull.

"We need to call the police," he says.

I nod.

An owl screeches nearby.

I look up through the branches and see the same owl that has sat on my window ledge. It peers at us, bobbing its head, almost as if nodding. It hoots, then flies off toward the house, and sits on Margaret's windowsill.

"It's Sawyer," I whisper. I have no idea where that thought comes from, but immediately I know it's true.

"I agree," Aiden says. He turns around and leads us out of the bushes. He stops and pulls out his cell phone, and is immediately talking, telling the police department's receptionist what we found.

He disconnects, and we stand there without saying a word. I grab his hand, and he squeezes, not letting go.

Amanda and Mars come out of the house as the police walk across the lawn. I hold up my hand when Amanda and Mars are about twenty feet in front of me to stop them. They do, and I join them.

The police follow Aiden into the bushes.

An hour later, as it gets dark, the body is removed.

Amanda and Mars went back into the house some time ago.

Aiden joins me, and we both continue to watch.

"What happens now?" I ask.

"He'll be taken to the big island where he'll be identified, and the cause of death will be determined."

"Aren't the remains mostly skeletal?"

"Yes, but they found a bullet beside the spine and where I imagine a major organ resided, like the liver or kidney." He turns to me. "Someone shot him."

Goosebumps. I know Aiden's right. "Did you tell them it's Sawyer?"

"Yes."

"But...?"

"One of them practically laughed, asking how could I know that? The other officer quickly chastised him, telling him to never rule out any possible evidence being provided."

"Evidence?"

"While not concrete, more police departments are using us. Mediums, psychics, intuitives. Science shows that the sixth sense is real."

"Who do you think killed him?"

"The same person who killed Margaret."

"Sawyer rang the bell," I blurt. It makes sense if Margaret was found up in the bedroom.

"I believe so, too. But, what doesn't make sense is how did Sawyer end up in the lilacs?"

We kick a few ideas around, but then exhaustion overwhelms me.

"You need to go to bed," Aiden tells me.

I yawn again and nod. It's been another long day, and the tension of finding Sawyer made it even longer. Stressful. And, I never had a chance to talk with Amanda.

Minutes later, I lay in bed, sinking into the mattress and pillows, hearing the lake's waves, the hoot of an owl, and then a whisper.

Trust him.

Chapter 60

Hunter

The next day, the workmen finish outside, repairing the house's stone foundation and replacing mortar where needed. They won't be coming back. The bathrooms and kitchen are finished, and the outside repaired. The house has been brought up to code.

Aiden was in Sinclair for most of the day. Mars, Amanda, and I spent the day cleaning: vacuuming, dusting, shining, rearranging furniture, bringing some pieces down from the attic, and hanging artwork.

It's late and everyone has gone to bed, including me. Even though it's cooled a bit tonight, my window is open partway.

An owl hoots. An occasional tree frog croaks. A breeze blows one of the curtains out. I half expect the lilac scent to accompany the breeze, but it doesn't. Is Margaret finally gone? I can't believe that she is.

I settle back against my pillows and pick up Margaret's diary. I'm near the end and feel sad that I'll have nothing more of hers to read. Especially knowing what lies ahead in her future.

She talks about the baby finally going to sleep, giving her a few minutes to write before Sawyer joins her. She writes about an owl carving and how Grandfather says it matches his box cover.

The owl box belonged to Grandfather? And, there's another carving?

I sit up no longer tired.

It's perfect by the bell. Even though we're living on different islands, having the carving is like having him here protecting me.

How could I have missed seeing a carving by the front door?

I grab the flashlight off my nightstand, not bothering with slippers or a covering for my pajamas. It's not like I expect anyone else to be up.

I don't want to wait until morning to look for it.

At the front door, I unlock it, and pull it open.

I cross the threshold, shut the door, and turn on the flashlight, moving the beam across the header.

Nothing.

I sweep the beam to the left and then to the right.

Nothing.

How can it not be there? Did I miss reading something?

I sweep the beam fully to the right, to the left, and then back to the right one more time.

Nothing.

I hear something behind me. Immediately, I click off the light and turn with my back to the door.

Searching through the landscape nearest me, I see nothing, so I peer further out, and include both sides of the porch, alongside the house and beyond. And then, I see it.

An owl. Sitting on a branch of the redbud tree that is off to the right of the porch and at the corner of the house. The tree had been planted halfway between the porch and the lilacs beyond it.

The owl and I stare at each other. It tilts its head, then swivels, so it's looking out onto the water. Likewise, my gaze goes toward the water. The owl continues to stare in that direction. Why?

I see movement by the shore. Or, am I imagining it? Black on black. And yet...

I hesitate, then pretend to go inside.

I open the door, step in, and start shutting the door but scooch down, almost crawling back out before shutting the door totally. I stay down.

Sure enough, whatever is out there is moving, but it's far enough away that I can't make out any details.

The owl hoots, then flies off. A scream like I've never heard before fills the air, then stops as if it's been muffled. The owl made an attack.

I stand up, still looking at the lawn toward the water. If there is anything out there, it isn't moving now. Is my imagination working overtime?

I go inside, determined to check for the owl carving in the morning.

Locking the door solidly behind me, I walk through the house and go to the back door to make sure it's locked, too.

It isn't.

I stick my head out the door for a second, then shut it quickly, locking it. That was a stupid move. What if someone had been just outside the door? They could have attacked me.

I stand there for a minute, listening.

Silence.

If there is someone outside, they're locked out now. I need to check the rest of the house. In fact, I'm going to check to make sure everyone is inside.

A silent bed check.

A few minutes later, I'm back in my room. Everyone is sleeping. Yes, I peeked in the rooms, and I don't regret doing it. I feel safer having checked.

Chapter 61

Anonymous

What is Hunter doing outside with a flashlight?

I sink to the ground, while watching the beam of light move back and forth across the front door's header. What is she looking for?

With my knee painfully on a rock, I move slightly. A twig snaps.

Hunter turns around and stares in my direction. I sink further, holding my breath.

And then, that darn owl flies straight at me and attacks me, scratching my neck. I muffle my scream. Stupid of me to vocalize, but damn, it hurt!

Then, Hunter pretends to go inside. What is she thinking? That no one can see her crawling back outside? She's fully exposed against the light from inside before she shuts the door. Not a smart move. Good thing it's me and not some random stranger.

I can't believe my luck when she finally gives up and goes inside.

Just as I round the back corner of the house, Hunter sticks her head out the back door. Fortunately, she's looking in the other direction first. I drop to the ground and turn my face away, scrunching down into my collar. Curling my fingers, I pull my arms deeper into my sleeves, so my hands are hidden. The hat covers my hair.

She must have hurried through the house to get to the back

door as quickly as she did.

The door closes and I get up. Just as I reach the door, I hear the click of the lock.

I curse silently.

Not a problem. While I can pick any lock. I just don't like doing it in the dark. My phone's dead, so I can't use its light. Not that I want to use its flashlight capability, but the home screen's dim light would have been helpful.

Now, I'll have to use memory muscles. Still, it isn't a problem. Not really. I've been in worse jams.

I wait a few minutes, making sure she's no longer in the hallway before I tackle the lock.

Minutes later, I enter the hallway, shut the door behind me, and stand still, listening.

Nothing but silence.

I creep upstairs and head to my room, not hearing anyone moving around. And then, I see a light at the end of the hall. The light goes out.

It's Hunter, and she's peeking into a room.

Is she checking everyone's room? Does she suspect one of us was outside?

Quickly, I'm in my room, remove my shoes, and pull back the covers revealing the pillowed dummy I had created. I climb in beside the pillows, so my back is to the door with the pillows hidden, blocked by my body.

It was stupid of me to go outside to make my phone call, ensuring no one could hear me. I couldn't take the chance of being heard. How many times have I overheard other people talking when we were in different rooms? These floor vents in almost every room are a curse. Why Hunter chose not to remove them is beyond me.

I wait a few minutes, hearing nothing. She must have peeked

into my room earlier.

Checking to make sure she's gone, I take a chance and open my door a crack.

Darkness and silence greet me.

I close the door and change my clothes, confident nothing is amiss.

Chapter 62

Hunter

First thing the next morning, I go to the front porch and inspect the door frame. I should have worn a jacket. A cold front came through last night, and the wind coming off the lake is chilly.

I see nothing at first, so I look again, more slowly this time, and expand my search outward a bit. Finally, I see it in the stone wall itself, situated near the bell. The owl carving Margaret had written about. Small, but an owl, with its wings outstretched and flying toward the observer.

Everything that I read in Margaret's diary has turned out to be true. I have no reason to doubt anything I've read so far or will read in the future.

Minutes later, I'm seated alone at the table in the dining room eating breakfast. Mars and Amanda enter the dining room. They're dressed in layers. Mars is carrying his jacket and hangs it on the back of his chair. Amanda is already wearing hers, her shoulders hunched, the collars flipped up almost to her chin. "Brrr. It got cold fast!" She's rubbing her crossed arms as she hugs herself. "What's winter going to be like?"

"An adventure," I say. I've got a scarf around my neck. If my neck is exposed, I'm cold; but if my neck is covered, I'm not. "Want one of my scarves to wrap around your neck," I ask her.

"No, I'll buy one in town." That's when they tell me they're going to the mainland to shop for needed supplies, including some groceries, hence the layers and jackets. We're low on just about everything.

They go into the kitchen and return a few minutes later with their breakfast and sit down.

"Do you have a list?" I ask.

Mars taps the piece of paper next to his plate. "We were just adding to it."

"Mind if I take it into the kitchen, just to double-check?" I ask.

"Go for it," he says, handing it to me.

I get up and move around the table. He stretches his arm out behind him with the list as I pass by. I stop seeing something on the back of his neck. I pull down his collar. "What's this? How'd you get that awful scratch?"

Quickly, he pulls his collar up, covering it. "Scraped up against something in my room, I guess," he says. "Stupid move. Wasn't looking where I was going."

"What were you doing?" Amanda asks.

He shrugs. "Who knows? Hunter, did you say you're doing laundry today?"

"Yes."

"Can you do mine?" he asks. "I'll go and—"

"That's okay," I say. "I'll get it when I bring mine down. Okay if I go into your room and get yours?"

"Sure."

"Mine, too!" Amanda says. "Just the clothes draped on the chair."

Minutes later, they go out the front door, headed for Sinclair, and I go up to collect our laundry.

I'm in Mars' room when I see a file folder on his bedside table with my name on it. He must have forgotten to put it away.

I debate whether to look inside. I shouldn't.

But, I can't help myself. "My house, my rules," I justify

aloud.

Though everything I already know from the family tree website is there. It appears he got the DNA results six months ago according to the paper I'm holding, and yet he had told Amanda and me that he got it about a week before my birthday.

The porch bell rings. I look up. It wasn't loud, and it rang only once. A half ding if that and not loud either. Like the clapper barely touched the bell.

I step to the window, the file still in my hand. There isn't any wind.

Did someone ring it to indicate danger? If so, why isn't it still ringing? Suddenly, I feel cold.

And then, I smell smoke.

Spinning around, black smoke streams out of the fireplace. How can that be? There isn't any fire.

It doesn't make sense.

I drop the file and run to the door.

It's locked!

I pound on the door heavily and start screaming.

The door opens, and Aiden rushes past me, opening the windows.

Immediately, the smoke is pulled out the windows and the room clears.

How can smoke that was pouring out one minute stop like that? Or even start?

"Are you all right?" Aiden asks.

"Yes, I think so. The smoke just started pouring out of the chimney. How is that even possible?"

"I don't know. It's a new one for me, too."

He frowns, looking down at my feet.

I look down, too, and see them. A toothpick.

Aiden picks it up and sniffs. "Whisky."

Running footsteps and the door opens, crashing against the wall.

Mars.

Breathing hard, he enters the room and stops, seeing the toothpicks in Aiden's hand. He frowns, then looks at me. "Are you okay? I heard you scream. I was coming back to—"

"Is this yours?" Aiden asks.

Mars looks confused.

"No. Yes.... Yes." he says. He takes it and sees the file on the floor.

Aiden steers me to the door. I look back and am surprised to see Mars glaring at me, but immediately his expression changes. It's his blank expression, the one I've seen him perform many times when he's been caught at something and is pretending total innocence. He can be quite the prankster with Amanda and me, especially Amanda. But, his favorite target in school had been teachers. Later, I watched him do it to strangers. Clerks. People in line.

He's good at it. Too good.

We leave the room.

Why was he glaring at me?

Or, was it at Aiden?

Chapter 63

Aiden

"Can you help me understand something?" Hunter asks. We just left Mars' room, heading for the stairs.

"Sure, what is it?"

She pulls me into her room and puts a finger to my lips to silence me. When I frown, she points to the floor vent nearby. I nod and point to the smaller connecting room that has become her closet. I know there aren't any vents in there.

She whispers, and I step closer to hear her. "That toothpick..." Her voice fades into silence as she looks at me, her gaze darting back and forth between my eyes and my mouth.

The tension in here is off the charts. Sexual tension. We've been avoiding it for the last couple of days, but now, this close, it's unavoidable. I want to kiss her but refrain. I want to continue collaborating with her and not let anything get in the way. Including my feelings. Or hers.

I can tell the moment she feels the sexual tension, as well. The air vibrates warmly around us.

This close, her eyes are mesmerizing. It's a mistake being this close, and yet, it's not. It's the most natural feeling in the world.

She takes a step back, but my hands wrap around her upper arms to stop her from leaving. I want to keep her near me.

"Don't go. I know why you want to leave, but don't go.... It's not a mistake."

She gasps. Obviously, she's surprised that I'm reading her mind. How can I not? How can she not be reading mine? Maybe she has been all along, and that's why she wants to put distance between us.

"Tell me why you brought me in here."

She takes a deep breath and blows it out, her lips forming an O. Later, I will kiss those lips, but not now. *Concentrate.* I let go and take a half step back to create just enough distance so she can focus, too.

"That toothpick," she whispers. "It wasn't there when I first went into the room. So, whose is it? You didn't drop it. Sawyer soaked his in bourbon."

"What about Mars?"

"He ran into the room when it was already on the floor. Think it could have already been there?" she asks.

"What's his booze preference?"

"Whisky."

"You must have missed seeing it. It's his room after all. Who else preferred whisky? Did you feel anything just before the smoke appeared?"

"Cold," she answered.

"Did you feel that cold when we saw Sawyer enter the lilacs?"

She frowns, her gaze at my chest, and looks up again in acknowledgment. "You know, every time I felt the cold, I was in the hallway off the kitchen. And when I saw Amanda being pushed—"

"Not to mention you being pushed, too," I add.

She nods. "Is Frank the cold?"

"Let's go down there, right now," I suggest. "Into the hallway and find out."

I take her hand, leading her out of her closet and across the room. At the door, she lets go of my hand, and we go downstairs.

Chapter 64*

Margaret

1922

Immediately upon returning home with Sawyer by my side, Grandfather ushers us to the dinner table. It's late, and he knew we'd be starving. As we eat, the entire shakedown of Frank and Mary's lies is revealed.

Sawyer is indeed Johnny—Jonathan Sawyer Van Houten. He'd gone by Johnny Van when at the logging camp as a boy. He'd been running away from an abusive school situation combined with gangs when Grandfather took him in. When Sawyer returned, even Grandfather didn't know who he was right away—not until Sawyer confided what was going on, enlisting Grandfather's help—and Father's.

A gambler who got himself into trouble from time-to-time playing cards with skilled card shark loggers, Father became Frank's underling, once Frank bought out the loggers' debts that Father couldn't possibly pay back.

"Sadly, your father never obtained the backbone he needed," Grandfather says, "Which is why I gave you the house and island to begin with and then the business. He'd have ruined it within a year."

I nod knowing Grandfather speaks the truth. I'd heard the gossip as a girl about Father's addiction to gambling, never understanding its reality back then.

Sawyer became an undercover U.S. Marshall, working his

way up the criminal chain until he was directly under Frank in Detroit. Once Frank moved, he was looking for a way to bring Sawyer with him and found it through me with Mary's help who became Frank's secret girlfriend. We were only teenagers then. We'd been close as kids, but as we grew older, she became my shadow, always nearby. I was captivated by her so-called devotion to me, all done via Frank's plan to become engaged to me and take over the business once we were married, no doubt only to get rid of me somehow. She had used me just as much as he had.

"I feel bad that I had to lie to you about that last locked door," Sawyer confesses. "I didn't want you knowing the room had stored illegal booze."

"You were part of Frank's operation while you in Harbor House?"

Sawyer nods.

"Why I needed you to be careful when delivering my message," Grandfather said.

"You were protecting Grandfather when he fired you," I said.

"And, your father. He was the true thief, but he was being blackmailed because of his gambling, and I didn't know how to help him. The three of you were a huge part of the reason why I became a U.S. Marshall."

*****

A week later, our wedding day is a marvelous gathering of townspeople and loggers. We couldn't wait.

Sawyer's best friend, a fellow Marshall from Detroit, serves as Sawyer's best man, and arrived with news that Frank and Mary had both been arrested. There's no doubt that they'll both be found guilty at their trials.

After the wedding, we honeymoon on Harbor House Island where I discover Sawyer has finished Grandmother's bedroom, redoing the attached room, which had been Grandmother's dressing room, turning it into a nursery.

We have plans.

Chapter 65*

Margaret's Diary

1924

I can't believe I've not written in over a year. A year and a half, actually.

I'm so happy! And so busy!

We've got a baby girl, and I sit here in the rocker to nurse. I just put her down for a nap but didn't want to leave the room yet, so I'm writing this, enjoying the view.

Sawyer owns and runs the business with me. Grandfather made it official shortly after the wedding. I do the bookwork from here, and Sawyer runs it mostly from Grandfather's house. He and Grandfather meet every day in Grandfather's office. I'm glad Grandfather's still alive and healthy, even if he doesn't get around as easily as he used to.

Because Father testified against Mary and Frank, he received a lighter sentence and was jailed, serving his time in a Detroit jail. Sadly, though, he died from the Spanish Flu epidemic that hit Detroit hard.

It was a tough time for everyone, including Grandfather, who doesn't leave the house anymore and enjoys Sawyer's company while educating him about the business.

Anytime Sawyer is on the dock, he waves at the house, knowing I'm probably in the nursery or bedroom, sitting in the rocking chair, nursing, watching the harbor and its doings.

I know it's silly and that he can't really see me, but I always wave back.

*****

For the last few days, I've had a sense of foreboding, but I can't attach the feeling to anything going on here in the house, on the island, or even in Sinclair.

And yet...

It feels like something evil is coming this way.

Chapter 66

Hunter

Present Day

Aiden brings me into the hallway off the kitchen, where the outside door opens to the east side of the island.

Putting my hand close to the wall, I move it around. Once I feel a whisper of air on my palm as before, I move my hand so Aiden can replace my hand with his. I watch as he moves his hand up and then across the wall. To me, his movement indicates there's a door of some kind.

Aiden stands back and examines the length of the wall, first to his left and then to his right, before staring at the wall in front of him.

Balling his hand, he pounds on the wall.

"What are you looking for?"

"A secret latch."

He pounds his fist against a few more spots.

CLICK.

A door pops open, but only an inch, if that.

"What's going on?"

Surprised, I turn my head. Mars comes down the steps and into the hall, with Amanda on his heels and Daisy behind her, though Daisy stands on the top step and cocks her head before following.

I say, "I thought you two were going to Sinclair." I don't like that they're here, witnessing our discovery.

Aiden pulls the door open. Daisy growls and backs away.

A musty odor fills the hall. Immediately, I cover my nose and mouth with my hand. Mold, no doubt. Amanda, having done the same, goes around us and open's the outside door. Fresh air sweeps through the hall, removing most of the smell.

Aiden lets go of the door; it starts to swing shut. He grabs it and holds it open. "Go get me a crowbar."

Mars runs up into the kitchen and returns a few seconds later with the tool in hand, giving it to Aiden, who jams it under the door, using it as a doorstop.

He pulls out his phone and turns on its light, shining it into the room. He steps inside.

I follow, needing to cover my nose again. The smell is so bad I can hardly breathe. The room is empty and extremely dark. There aren't any windows, no other entrance.

Why does it smell so bad in here? Because it's been locked up for one-hundred years?

Mars turns on a flashlight and with hurried steps, moves around us, attempting to go deeper into the room.

Aiden grabs his arm, stopping him, and asks, "What are you looking for?"

Amanda is behind me now. Daisy stands in the doorway and continues to growl.

Mars' gaze darts around, his concentration on the walls. "Nothing. It's just—"

"What's that?!" Amanda points to the ground just ahead of us.

Aiden swings the beam of light in the direction Amanda is pointing.

Rotted material and a badly decomposed body that is mostly bones. Near one hand, a gun.

"Everyone out! Now!" I demand.

Mars hesitates, looking toward one of the walls again.

"You, too, Mars," Aiden says.

Amanda and I reach the hall first. Mars follows, and Aiden stands in the doorway.

Mars, Amanda, and I listen while Aiden calls the police. When he hangs up, he says, "They said no one is to go in."

We traipse up the stairs into the kitchen, where I shut the kitchen door to the hallway, and then we go into the adjoining dining room and sit.

"How long before they're here?" Amanda asks.

"Twenty minutes at most," Aiden replies.

"Anyone want something to drink?" I ask, getting up. "There's some juice in the fridge."

The others say no, but I need to be doing something. A minute later, I return with four glasses.

Mars is gone. I hand Aiden and Amanda theirs. "Where's Mars?"

"He said he was going to wait outside. That he needed some fresh air," Amanda responds.

Fresh air sounds good, but I want to finish my drink first.

"Who do you think it is?" Amanda asks.

I glance at Aiden and he at me. We both know.

It's Frank.

"Don't know," Aiden says.

"I don't know either," I say. To Aiden, I ask, "If there was a tiny bit of air escaping through the wall, how could the room smell so badly? If he's been in there for a century, wouldn't there be no odor?"

Amanda gasps. "He? A century? You know who it is!"

Aiden replies, "We're only surmising. We don't know for sure."

To quiet Amanda's anxiety and to stop her barrage of questions, I finally say, "We think it's Frank Darnell."

Immediately, she shuts up and looks down at her hands, which are in her lap, and which I notice are clenched tightly together. She knows something.

Just then, the police arrive. I'm not able to question her about what she knows.

Strange that Mars didn't follow them in.

Aiden leads the men to the kitchen, with Amanda and me following.

When Aiden opens the hall door, immediately I see that the back door is open. Still open. We hadn't shut it.

The police plug a long cord connected to a huge circle searchlight into a kitchen outlet and place the light inside the room. Immediately, it's like day in there.

Aiden, Amanda, and I stay in the hall as they investigate.

Aiden points to the body. "The body wasn't like that when we found it. Someone's been in here."

One policeman exits the room and heads straight outdoors. He comes running back announcing, "A small boat is racing toward Canada."

I run through the house and look out the front door. My boat is gone!

Running around to the back of the house, I overhear one officer radioing the Canadian police force. The boat thief will be apprehended before he ever makes landfall.

It has to be Mars. He's the only one missing.

Part II

Chapter 67*

Frank Darnell

1924

Despite working in the dark, it takes him only a minute to pick the lock of the lower-level back door that leads to the storeroom. He remembers it well.

He doesn't want to turn on his flashlight until he is inside and assured that he is alone. He's here via a Canadian tugboat that will be gone if he takes longer than an hour.

No problem. He plans to be back in the dinghy rowing to the tug waiting offshore in less than fifteen minutes.

He approached the island from the Canadian side so that no one on the Sinclair docks could see him. He doubts anyone is on the docks, but he isn't taking any chances.

Jailed since the end of 1922, he recently escaped, and has no plans of returning.

If anyone is in the house, they'll be asleep. He hopes no one is in the house, but just in case, that's why the tug crossed the lake with no lights and why he was entering through the back entrance, which was the hallway where the lower-level storeroom was located. And, his money.

Opening the door just wide enough to slither through, he steps onto a dirt floor hallway and quickly but quietly shuts the door, not letting it latch shut. He wants an easy escape.

He stands there listening.

All is quiet.

Turning on his flashlight, he illuminates the wall.

Where's the door?!?

There used to be a door here!

He swings the light to the opposite wall.

No door.

He's sure he's remembering correctly. He steps midway in the hall, to where the door should have been. He walked this hall many times back when he was living in Sinclair and would sneak onto the island to oversee incoming shipments of the illegal booze stored here before being distributed to ports down Lake Huron between here and Detroit.

When Margaret returned to Sinclair and they were engaged, he had to pretend he'd never been on Harbor House Island or in the house.

He beams the light in every direction, trying to find a crack somewhere, a sliver of space that will reveal a door.

Not finding any, he reacts, pounding the wall.

CLICK.

The door unlatches and pops out half an inch.

A gasp sounds.

He turns his head. He sees the tail end of a skirt or robe before it disappears.

Quickly, he slides the bag off his shoulder and down his arm, to the ground, then leaps all three steps at once.

He stumbles and drops the flashlight. It goes out.

Pitch black.

Running footsteps in another room. Running away from him.

He curses and starts feeling around for the flashlight. Too much time is passing. They're getting away.

But, to where? There's nowhere to go.

Finally, his fingers feel the round cylinder. He grabs it and clicks it on. Nothing.

He curses again, hitting it against the wall. It still doesn't come on.

He hits it against the wall again. Finally, it comes on.

Scrambling to his feet, he gives chase, running through the dining room, around the dining room table and chairs, through the parlor, and out into the great hall.

Directing his light up the stairs, he sees her.

Margaret.

Up on the landing, she looks. Horror on her face as she recognizes him. She disappears.

He tears up the stairs, taking two and three steps at a time.

On the landing, he sees a dim light down one hall. A door slams. The hall is dark.

He runs down the hall and stops at the closed door, twisting the knob.

Locked.

He slams up against the door.

The door frame splinters.

Margaret faces him with a small gun in her hand.

He races toward her.

She fires just as he reaches her, knocking her arm up. The gun fires at the ceiling.

Bits of plaster fall on them.

He pushes her hard against the bedpost.

A sickening thud, but she doesn't go down.

He grabs her with one hand. She struggles to get away. He pulls his knife out with his other hand, slashing her throat.

She falls to the floor, blood sliding down her neck and fanning out underneath her long, curly hair.

Moving out of the room, he's on the stair landing when he hears the front door opening and someone coming in.

Quickly, he turns off his light.

Looking down, he sees Sawyer looking up at him.

He didn't turn the light off quickly enough.

Pulling his gun out of his belt, he shoots at Sawyer.

Sawyer turns and runs out the front door.

Before Frank can get to the front door, he hears the big bell by the front door—the emergency bell—being rung.

In two more steps, Frank is outside and pushes Sawyer down the stairs.

Sawyer doesn't get up. Frank flies down the steps and flips him over. His abdomen is red with blood.

Good! The bullet found its mark, after all. He feels for a pulse.

There isn't one.

Frantic that he's been seen, he looks up. Because of the fog, he can barely see this dock. No one in Sinclair would have seen him.

Move!

If there is anyone on Sinclair's docks, he's only got twenty minutes at most before they're landing here, responding to the bell.

He grabs Sawyer's collar and drags him into the lilac bushes, quickly covering him with decades of debris. He grabs a limb and retraces his steps, scraping the ground, hoping no one will notice the disturbance.

Suddenly, the wind stirs, and it's raining again. He discards the branch in such a way that it looks like it was blown there. *The rain will hide everything.*

He lifts a foot to climb the stairs, but hesitates. *Don't leave tracks.*

He takes off his boots and carries them, returning to the kitchen, then the hallway, before putting his boots back on. Only then does he step onto the dirt floor hallway.

He inserts his fingers into the exposed crack. His flashlight goes out again. *Cursed torch!*

Banging it against the wall, it comes on again.

He pulls the door open. *Clever.* The former frame is gone. The entire opening has been made into a hidden door that becomes part of the wall when closed. As if they don't want anyone to ever know it's there.

He goes inside and isn't surprised to find the room empty. The liquor barrels would have been removed.

Frank beams the light onto the floor, turning it toward the outer wall, where he had buried the money. With the barrels gone, he has to rely on his memory. Picturing the rows, he can gauge the distance between them. Hopefully, he's making an educated guess. At worst, he's guessing. Go down the fifth row until reaching the wall. He buried between the fifth and sixth rows, in the small space between the rows and the wall.

In just a few minutes, he's made a few holes with his hands. Nothing.

Where is the bag?

Panicked, he digs furiously.

Finally, he finds it!

Clutching it, he rises.

CLICK!

Startled, he grabs the light and goes to the door. It's shut.

He pushes on it, but it won't give.

There isn't a handle anywhere. *Every door has a handle, a way to open it, doesn't it?*

His flashlight goes out again. Cursing, he strikes it against the door, but it won't turn on no matter how many times he beats it again the wall.

Angry, he drops it and starts feeling the door and the

surrounding wall, feeling for a button or switch. There has to be a way to open the door.

He hears the bell ringing. Even in this tightly closed room, the sound reverberates.

How can it be ringing when he killed them both?

Who's ringing it?

*****

An hour later, the place is swarming with police and FBI. They'd been getting into position for a raid elsewhere on the big island, amassing secretly in various locations. They'd been contacted by Sawyer's foreman, who had found Margaret's body.

Even though Frank Darnell's operation had been shut down, others had sprung up elsewhere. No one wanted prohibition repealed more than these agents who'd been fighting the rise of organized crime in these small northern communities, where there'd been a steady rise of stills built in the backwoods.

Standing in the dining room, Martin Strand says to his partner, Timothy Green, "Do you hear that?"

"What?"

"A knocking sound."

They listen. Sounds of other officers in other rooms talking and moving are heard.

"I don't hear any knocking," Timothy says. "Sounds like the wind has picked up."

Martin strains to listen. "You're right. I just refastened one shutter. No doubt the wind is whipping another shutter somewhere."

*****

The next day, an official report is filed.

Margaret Sinclair Van Houten was found murdered in her bedroom with her throat slashed. Sawyer Van Houten, her husband, is missing. Their baby, who had been asleep in the nursery, is the only survivor of the tragedy and is with a step-relative, as there are no other living relatives.

Margaret Sinclair's grandfather, George Sinclair, founder of Sinclair, died just hours after learning his granddaughter had been murdered.

An APB bulletin alert has been made for Jonathan Sawyer Van Houten. No one else is suspected at this time.

Chapter 68

Mars

Present Day

I came from a tough neighborhood and an even tougher family. What we won't do for a few dollars.

I grew up listening to my grandfather, Antonio, talk about how he was the secret baby of Edward Sinclair and Frank's sister and should have inherited the Sinclair fortune.

He would tell stories, too, about his Uncle Frank and repeat his exploits of bootlegging, and how long he got away with it under the nose of the elder Sinclair, Margaret's grandfather. He always laughed when talking about Frank how when engaged to Margaret, his secret girlfriend, Mary—Margaret's best friend in boarding school—screwed things up. How Frank and Mary both ended up in jail.

Frank didn't stay there long. Less than two years later, he escaped and was never heard from again.

Growing up listening to those stories, I didn't believe half of them. Not until I started doing some online research just before Grandpa Antonio started getting Alzheimer's and then died less than a year later when I was graduating from high school.

I had no proof of his stories, but hearing about the money, I was determined to find proof.

Shortly after that, my parents were arrested. I got lost in the system and made sure no one could find me. I changed my name to Mars Smith and made myself a few years younger. I was skinny and looked younger than I was. I had learned about Hunter through my computer sleuthing. All I knew was that she was adopted, a Sinclair by blood, and had just finished her first year of high school.

I found and rented a cheap studio apartment from an older, single woman who didn't require a background check if I paid cash. She was as crooked as I was, so we helped each other along the way. She was my aunt according to my school records, and I was her nephew, a dependent, whenever it meant she could receive extra funds elsewhere. Never on tax records, though. Neither of us was that stupid.

I was hiding in plain sight.

I started creating some family trees on ancestor websites using fictitious names via email accounts, making a few of the trees public, but not the most important one. It remained private. I was after the research from the trees of others. Especially those that could link up with the Darnell family. That's how I learned about Hunter.

I pretended having moved to the area and being in the ninth grade, joining the class the last few weeks of the second semester, allowing me to meet Amanda first, and then a week later, Hunter.

I made sure that we became fast friends.

I never went back to the old neighborhood. I stayed close to my apartment, never going out much at night. Just school and home, plus some easy nighttime thefts, making sure I never left a trail of any kind.

People are fooled so easily. They trust just about everyone.

After graduation, I was able to get into a good college across the country because of my computer skills. I took the opportunity and did well, getting referral letters from my professors.

I returned to Detroit a new man, muscled and with

legitimate skills. Amanda and Hunter barely recognized me.

Once I was back, I concentrated on my work, most of which I could do from home. But, a couple years later I was broke. I was desperate, so I robbed a few homes. I'd do it after announcing I was going away, then sneak back, make the robbery, and sneak back out of town, returning normally a couple days later. I was selling any merchandise I collected. But, it wasn't going well. Times were tough.

Amanda and Hunter were almost done with college having pursued their masters.

That's when I remembered Hunter's mom's jade collection. I hadn't planned on killing them. I was shocked to find them home. They were shocked seeing me. I had no choice.

Thankfully, I sold the collection on the black market—save one piece a warrior, because it symbolized the meaning of my new name: Mars. From the first time I had seen that jade piece, I wanted it. After I got it, I tucked it behind some books. I could see it when at my desk and only at my desk, but if I was in front of that bookcase, it was hidden.

Later, I realized her parents being gone could work to my benefit. With them dead, I figured she'd discover revealing papers about her adoption. No such luck. To this day, their deaths are an unsolved mystery. And, she never found any papers.

At first, I felt a bit guilty but not for long. I was happy that Hunter depended on her two friends. We made her feel safe.

And then finally, six months before her birthday, not able to wait any longer, I created an online ancestry account in her name, building it legitimately, mimicking the moves anyone would make having just created an account. Only recently was I able to create the links to the Sinclair family.

My ultimate goal: I wanted the money Grandpa Antonio bragged about. Money that Frank had hidden, letting the FBI believe it was gone.

The only way I could get access to the house was to get access through Hunter.

One thing I had learned about criminal activities, I heard from stories told about Frank: He took his time, making long-range goals.

Amanda and Hunter believe my businesses are doing well. I'm great at selling the lie. Any lie. Multiple lies.

Everything was going well until that day Amanda saw my open computer and my own family tree. When she saw that both Hunter and I were related to the Sinclair family, she convinced me to start an account for Hunter. She had no idea; I already had.

One day, while I was with Hunter and Amanda, my apartment was broken into. Strangely enough, I didn't lose my laptop or anything electronic, other than my gaming equipment. I figured it had to have been a teenage boy or two in the neighborhood. My hidden camera revealed it was only one person, and it looked like one of those boys. But, I didn't dare report the robbery because I didn't want anyone discovering who I really was, so I just replaced the equipment that was stolen.

It wasn't until much later that I discovered that the piece of jade had been stolen, too.

Now, I'm on my way to Canada. I snuck around to the back of the house while they sat like stooges waiting for the police.

I found the money under Frank's body. It was disgusting having to touch him, and the bag disintegrated as I moved it. So, I took off my shirt, using it as a bag.

I was able to sneak around and get Hunter's boat without being seen. It's chilly out here on the lake without a coat or a shirt, but I'll be on land quick enough and can buy what I need.

Chapter 69

Hunter

In the beginning, I was angry. I was just finishing my freshman year of high school when I learned I was adopted.

I had a habit of staying up reading. Often, when my parents were up late watching television, I'd hear snatches of conversation that sounded more like rumblings than words. The stairwell acted like a megaphone of sorts—not loudly, but with nuances and a few words now and then. If I crawled out into the hall, I could hear them clearly.

On that one night, I heard words I wish I hadn't. I should have stayed in my room.

The TV was off, and their conversation sounded serious.

Having heard various kids talking in the past about their parents divorcing and how it came as a shock to some of them, I didn't want to be caught unaware.

I had crept out of my bedroom and was lying on the floor at the top of the stairs. I couldn't see them or they me.

Dad must have been in his rocker—a cloth chair much like a recliner, but instead of reclining, it rocked. And swiveled. He liked that. Mom would always sit on the couch next to his chair, with a small end table between them with a lamp they used for reading.

"We need to tell her," Mom said.

"No, we don't," he replied. "We don't have to tell her anything. She's *our* daughter."

"But, what if someone else in the family speaks out of turn."

"Like my father? He's clamped shut tighter than a casket. Nothing's getting out of that man. What other family is there?"

In my mind's eye, I could see Mom shrugging her shoulders, like she does when she knows she doesn't have a good answer.

"No one else knows," he said. "We were careful about the arrangements."

"That's true."

"We went away telling people you were pregnant, and when we came back—"

"We had our baby girl," she finished.

"No one is ever going to know she isn't ours by birth."

Wait? What? I was adopted?

Horrified, I scooted back into my room and quietly shut the door.

I didn't sleep much that night.

I kept debating whether I should ask them about being adopted—but if I did that, then they'd know I'd been listening. Eavesdropping, and they wouldn't like that.

I wanted to know more. But, how to find out?

*****

I pondered the problem the entire next day.

The following morning, I woke up knowing what I would do. Instead of taking art or band as I did this past year, I'd take a computer class and learn how to really sleuth. We were all in the gym, lined up to register for classes next year. A last week activity.

That's when I met Mars and Amanda. She was behind me. Mars was beside me in another line.

It was finally my turn, and I was hesitating, considering which classes to take. That's when Mars reached over and signed me up for the same class as him.

Finished, I stepped back. Amanda stepped forward and he had her sign up for the same class.

Mars was taking as many computer classes as allowed. If he knew computers, he'd be a good friend to have. It's why I didn't fight his signing me up like that.

Right after we were done, I learned he and Amanda had met the week before, and he already knew he wanted a career involving computers, writing apps, and games.

I learned Amanda was sweet on him. I wondered how long that would last considering he always only saw her as a friend. But, she told me she was biding her time, waiting for him to notice her. She would have been a great girlfriend. It was sad that she wouldn't look elsewhere.

Like me, Amanda wanted to be a librarian, but she preferred being an IT technical librarian to my wanting to be a traditional public librarian. I wanted to be involved with book clubs and other literary activities for adults rather than for kids.

Amanda would make good use of the computer and IT classes she took with Mars.

Computers weren't my passion. Books were. Computers were merely a tool. Books are where I learn and armchair travel to other places.

I did great in the computer class, but I didn't have the same passion those two did. I found the class easy, including learning new programs, doing research, and creating apps. Everything. Truthfully, the lessons were boring. I did a semester's worth of work in just a couple weeks, so why take more classes when I could just as easily learn on my own?

Secretly, I bought their class books online and learned on my own, and was applying what I learned online in real time and practiced under a pseudonym.

Since I didn't take part in after-school activities, I was usually in my room after school and online. My parents loved how I was studying.

They had no idea.

I never told anyone about my adoption. I never wrote about it in my diary either. A diary Mom was reading.

One time, I wrote I had a crush on Mars, just to see if she'd say anything. She did. A few days later that she was telling me a story about two friends she had who lost their friendship because they both had a crush on the same boy.

When she asked, "*Did you know that Amanda has a crush on Mars?*" that's when I knew she'd read my diary. I told her I knew, and that I wasn't interested in him. You should have seen the puzzling look she gave me. *That'll teach her*, I thought at the time. But no, it ended up teaching me to be careful with who you trust.

Thanks to Mom and Dad, I had my own computer—they felt it was needed if I was serious about going to college, which I was. I knew I'd need a master's degree to become a librarian, so Dad offered to help with my math and sciences classes, which I appreciated, and Mom who was as much a reader as I was, read the books I was reading, and we'd talk about them.

Our discussions actually helped me when it came to tests and the SAT. She was deepening my critical-thinking skills.

She had no idea I was using those skills online as I learned about the Sinclair family.

I loved my parents. They were good to me and were wonderful role models, but I didn't trust them anymore. Were they afraid that I would desert them or hate them?

Our friendship too new, I kept my online searches a secret from Amanda and Mars. When I should have been able to trust, I couldn't. There were too many tiny lies I'd catch them in, never revealing what I knew. I followed the saying of keeping your friends close and your enemies closer. I wasn't sure if they were really my friends or just pretended to be.

Once I got through the class books that Amanda and Mars were assigned in their computer classes, I went on to college textbooks. I became more skilled than the two of them.

I browsed anonymously and stripped my computer clean of searches and anything that could be deemed suspicious every night. I kept all my research, communications, and anything else connected to my fake adult identity in a hidden file, including my bookmarks of website accounts, which included my privatized DNA results.

Even if my parents performed a search on my computer, they'd never find anything.

My parents were killed just before I graduated with my master's degree. A week after their burial, I graduated and drove the scenic route home rather than flying back with Amanda.

We'd gone to the same Minnesota university, and I was driving back to Detroit via the U.P., the Upper Peninsula, and then down along the Lake Huron coastline.

What she didn't know is that I was stopping in Sinclair.

I got onto Harbor House Island and into the house under the pretense of being an insurance adjuster because my company was reviewing its files.

I made arrangements to have keys left on the island, so I could pick them up without anyone seeing me. At first, I was surprised that no one wanted to meet me, but I figured this was probably routine throughout the years, so no one thought differently.

I was careful not to open any drawers or closets. Just a quick walk-through. There could have been hidden cameras, and I wasn't taking any chances. Once onshore again and in my car, I didn't stay. No one ever knew about my trip to Harbor House Island.

Driving home to Detroit back then, I knew for sure that one

day I would live there and fulfill my dream of having a B&B. Even though I talked about it to both Mars and Amanda abstractly, I knew exactly where it would be. It was just a matter of when.

Once I got home, I was dealing with my parents' estate and had to put my dream aside.

My parents didn't leave me much beyond the house and their car, which I sold since I already had one. That sale basically paid the probate taxes and part of their funeral expenses. Their life insurance, what little there was, paid for the rest.

Thankfully, since the house was paid for, my new library job paid the monthly expenses and let me save a little toward my B&B.

I concentrated on my job and fixing things in the house my father had delayed. Life went on, and my Sinclair connection remained on the back burner.

Until that one afternoon about six months ago when everything changed.

I remember that day clearly.

I sat at the kitchen table with the windows open a crack, with winter almost gone, enjoying a few days off work.

It'd been a while since I'd been on the ancestor websites, so I was visiting them all, checking out all the new stars I'd received over time. That's when I got a notification about another new connection.

Clicking it, I was taken to Mars' family tree and saw that his grandfather was Antonio Darnell.

Where had I heard that name before?

I took a screenshot.

Good thing I did because the link disappeared seconds later.

That's when I started digging into Antonio's background and discovered Mars was his grandson.

I was shocked.

Had he pretended to be my friend all this time because of our mutual connection to the Sinclair family? Sure seems like it. And, what about Amanda? How did she play into this?

Now, I didn't trust either of them, but I couldn't just kick them out of my life without cause.

Oh, I had plenty of cause but none I wanted to disclose.

Knowing Mars, he wouldn't be able to sit on this information forever. Eventually, he was going to let me know who I really was. I wondered how he'd do it.

I didn't have to wait long.

I managed to put a bug into Mars' computer that allowed me to track his keystrokes a bit earlier. It's how I learned he's a petty thief.

One day I saw an email account being made in my name, followed by the account being used to create an ancestor tree on the same website where I had submitted my DNA. He made the tree private, and I watched as he slowly built it.

What was taking him so long to show me? What was he waiting for? And what about Amanda? What did she know?

Little by little, I tested them both. I made throwaway innuendos. A few times, I caught them glancing at each other with a brief questioning as if to ask, *I didn't say anything, did you?*

Then they'd laugh it off, making whatever it was I had said a joke, telling me what a great sense of humor I had.

I was still trying to figure out how to get up to Harbor House Island when Mars outed me with my birthday present. Mars even contacted the trust folks in Sinclair anonymously with a link to the tree he had created that was listed as mine.

I had no idea about the trust once I discovered my Sinclair connection. Had I known, I would have outed myself earlier, but the timing was actually better this way.

The storm allowed me to dump my life in Detroit.

So, when Drew told me they had discovered the link themselves, I knew that was a lie. Wasn't anyone truthful anymore?

I had seen Mars send an email with the tree's link to a law firm in Sinclair, but I had no idea why. How he had known about the trust, I have no idea. Even in my research, my inheritance was a complete surprise. Had he been just as surprised?

My plan to use Amanda and Mars had finally arrived. Since Mars was secretly determined to get up there, they were going to be free labor as I renovated the house.

While I had told Amanda and Mars that I was putting my belongings in storage in Detroit while I went up to Harbor House for a couple weeks, in truth, everything was shipped up here and put in storage on Drummond Island. I was never going back to Detroit. I pretended about being indecisive.

I had enjoyed growing up and working at the library in Detroit, but Harbor House was home—my true family's home. It definitely feels like home now, more so with the mystery solved.

Swayer had never left, and evidence will prove that Frank had killed both, since his knife and gun were found beside his body.

I'm having that room sealed permanently.

The research I had performed during the last decade was immense, but it painted a complete picture of that time period, providing information about all the players—Frank, Mary, Sawyer, Margaret, her father, and her grandfather. Including her engagement to Frank, and then her marriage to Sawyer.

After that, there was no reporting until Frank broke out of jail, and then Margaret's murder and Sawyer's disappearance.

One report suggested that there was a huge chunk of money missing from a company Frank had done business with, and which had been connected to Frank's bootlegging. I suspected that was why Mars wanted to come north with me. I knew his businesses were failing and that he was looking for other work on the West Coast.

He wanted to search for the money and why I never questioned his shenanigans while he was here. I wanted him to find it.

Sure enough, thanks to Mars, we found Frank and the money. I could have pressed charges against Mars, but I didn't.

While the police were dealing with their observations and inquiry on Harbor House Island that day of Frank's discovery, Amanda told me she was leaving.

There was no stopping her this time.

She left with the police. They boated her over to Sinclair's dock where she planned to drive across the island, ferry to the mainland, and drive home.

I wished her well, doubting we'll ever be friends again.

Which brings me to now.

Aiden and I talked about the ghosts. We determined Frank was the pusher—pushing me and Amanda—and was the cold spot we felt. Reasonably, he could have been responsible for the choking black smoke that came out of the chimney, too.

Daisy's lockup will forever remain a mystery. I'll never know for sure who did it. While she never straight out accused Mars, Amanda reminded me how much he detested the dog.

We decided that the owl, the way it was always at the window, was Grandfather, as a protector.

Aiden and I stand on the dock, finally alone on the island. Amanda and the police having reached Sinclair's shores.

He turns me so I'm facing him. "I've been wanting to ask you this ever since I met you but decided you needed to get to know me first."

"And trust you," I inject.

He smiles. "Can we date?"

I answer, wrapping my arms around his neck, pulling him down so I can kiss him.

Chapter 70

Anonymous / Amanda

I hated that dog of hers. Even as I was leaving, it was barking and running around the yard, making a nuisance of itself. The only day there was peace and quiet in the house was the day I shut her in the bathroom.

Once the chaos of discovering Frank's body, Mars leaving, and then learning he was getting captured while still on Lake Huron died down enough for me to tell Hunter I was leaving, I packed my bag and got a boat ride back to Drummond Island with the police. Driving my car across the island, I only had to wait twenty minutes for the next ferry.

I wanted to leave without fanfare. Thankfully, Hunter was so preoccupied, she said she'd call me later and thanked me for coming.

An hour later, I'm on my way back home to Detroit.

I rub the scratches on the back of my neck where that stupid owl had clawed me.

Once they find the missing jade piece buried deep in Mars' luggage, he'll be arrested and returned to Detroit to be tried for the murders of Hunter's parents. Hunter will be completely shocked. That's when she'll call me, asking me if I knew anything about it. I'll tell her I'm just as surprised as she is.

But, I do know.

Mars thinks he's so smart.

I waited a long time to exact revenge. I needed him to find the treasure to spring my trap. He'll never know it was me.

I'm smarter than both of them, actually. They just don't know it.

I'm glad to be rid of that snippy little dog that I'd hidden in the bathroom, hoping Mars would be blamed. He hadn't been, so I implicated him just before I left. I always enjoyed his misery whenever Daisy went after him.

Long ago, I learned that Mars never truly empties his luggage when returning from trips. He has certain items he keeps in it, so he doesn't have to repack them every time. I had an opportunity to put the jade warrior in his luggage while we stayed at Harbor House, burying it where he wouldn't see it until he got home, wrapping it in material that would set off Xray and scanning machines. Of course, my plan was that he would never make it home.

But, since he's going to be arrested before he ever hits the Canadian shoreline, they'll go through his luggage thoroughly once his luggage catches up to him. No doubt, discovering the murderer of Hunter's parents will become big news.

In our computer classes, I played dumb and was always asking for his help. Consequently, he let me into his life. It was so easy. Such a stooge. He let me into his awful apartment, too, quite often. I was ever so grateful when he returned from college and moved into something much nicer.

Oh, nothing ever happened, other than him sharing computer tips with me, eating pizza ordered in. Always my treat. I knew how poor he was. I always brought some whisky; he hated bourbon. His drinks would be full strength; mine were diluted. He loved being waited on.

I knew everything about him. His fake name. His many projects. He had more scams going than most women have shoes.

How did I know? We'd drink on those pizza nights, and he'd tell me everything, not remembering a bit of what he had told me the next day. The more I learned, the more pizza nights we began having.

He taught me how to pick locks, too. He was so proud of his skills, telling me of different robberies no one knew about and then forgetting he'd told me.

When I saw the jade warrior behind his favorite books, I knew right then that he had murdered Hunter's folks. Hunter's mom was proud of her jade collection. She'd show it to me every time I visited. It'd been insured, too. The entire collection had been stolen.

When I questioned him about it during one of our next pizza/drinking get-togethers, once I was sure he was drunk almost to the point of passing out, he revealed he hadn't meant to kill them. He thought they were gone from the house. He had snuck in the front door and left by the back door because the snoopy neighbor across the street was sitting on his front porch. That's when he realized they'd seen him. He wasn't safe, so he had no choice. He killed them. He confided in the end that killing them sped up his plan to get Hunter up to the island.

Early on in my friendship with Mars, I cloned his computer so I could watch everything he did, right down to the keystrokes of his passwords. I wrote my own programs, enabling me to spy on him. I was even able to watch him through his own cameras he had installed for security reasons.

He never knew. I could have won an acting award. So many performances.

The first time I saw his family tree online, I couldn't figure out what he was doing until I heard him talking on the phone with his grandfather via his camera.

I knew exactly when Hunter first discovered she was adopted. It was through a handwritten class assignment that we each submitted anonymously. They'd been collected, shuffled, and then handed out for critiquing without knowing whose was whose.

Except I did. I recognized Hunter's handwriting. She wrote about discovering she was adopted.

Poor thing.

Not really.

I wanted to feel sorry for Hunter for losing her parents—who I already knew were adopted parents—but I didn't. I was miffed at her for never telling me she was adopted. Here I thought we'd been the best of friends. Obviously not.

And then later, thanks to my spyware, I heard Mars brag to his grandfather about how he was going to get Frank's money that was hidden inside Harbor House. He'd been fondling the piece of jade while he talked, so it had to have been shortly after the murder.

It was so easy setting up a meeting for the three of us, since I usually was the one who set them up. On that particular day, I was waiting outside of his apartment. I decided not to disable his cameras but to disguise myself instead. Let him think it was someone else.

The minute he left, I went in, made it purposely look like a robbery, stealing the jade and his favorite gaming equipment.

I was in and out in under a minute. I knew ahead of time what I'd be stealing and tossing a few things to make it look like a real burglary.

Just after I walked out of the building, I shed the hoodie and gave it to a homeless person who sat on the sidewalk along my short walk to the restaurant.

Technically, I was following Mars to the restaurant. Had he turned around, he might have seen me in the distance, but he never did.

He never noticed me. Not really.

The coup de grâce was my arrival at the restaurant just half a minute after the two of them had arrived.

When I learned about Hunter's inheritance, I really despised her then. Hating her even more when she was treated like royalty in Sinclair.

I put the stolen jade piece, which had some of Hunter's mother's DNA on it, in the bottom of his suitcase after we arrived on the island. Though it wouldn't have his own fingerprints on it because he would have wiped it clean before putting it on the shelf. He could be such a germophobe sometimes.

He'll have years in prison to wonder how her DNA got on it. During the trial, he'll learn how in the crevices, where the DNA was found, that the jade wasn't as clean as he thought.

He was so easy to manipulate. Any idea I suggested, I let him take ownership of it, letting him believe it'd been his idea to start with.

I'd been wanting revenge on Mars for a long time.

The boy is going to jail. For the rest of his life.

He should have paid attention to me.

Hunter?

I pushed her and don't regret it for a minute. Though, I have no idea who pushed me. Hunter had been across the room when it happened.

I planted the smoke bomb in Mars' room, too. It went off with a motion detector. My goal was to spook him. Even better was when Hunter got caught in the trap.

She'd been nothing but pure entertainment.

A plaything.

Like a cat with a mouse.

Time to find a new mouse.

Chapter 71

Hunter

Two Weeks Later...

Aiden carries me from the dock, past the Harbor House Bed and Breakfast sign and up the steps, setting me down on the landing.

"Want to ring the bell, Mrs. Grey?"

"I'd love to, but it's for danger."

"Not today. I warned everyone that it was going to ring in celebration today."

"Really?" I ask, grinning.

He nods.

It'd been a whirlwind two weeks where Aiden stayed, helping me prepare the house not only as a B&B but as a retreat several times a year for those who wanted to develop their psychic powers, intuition, how to communicate with those on the other side, and a secondary retreat to help those dealing with discovering they were adopted. Already, we're booked for both retreats for the upcoming winter months and into the spring and summer. And, we're filling up fast for winter enthusiasts who just want to get away and enjoy a peaceful winter vacation.

During those two weeks we finished fixing up the house, we became intimate lovers.

My fear of not having guests during the cold, winter months has disappeared.

I reach up and ring the bell.

Over in Sinclair, people on the docks wave and cheer.

"Look!" Aiden points at the lilac bushes.

The faint forms of Sawyer and Margaret, smiling at each other, walk toward the lake and into the last rays of sunlight, holding hands.

They reach the water with an owl following them, and the three of them disappear into the fading sunset.

About the Author

Diana Stout, MFA, Ph.D. writes fiction and nonfiction that blend compelling storytelling with practical insight. Her suspense, romance, and emotionally layered drama explore resilience, reinvention, and second chances, while her nonfiction simplifies mindset and habit science into clear, actionable tools. Her goal is simple: leave readers feeling stronger, more grounded, and inspired to create their next chapter.

Dr. Diana is an award-winning writer, who returned to school as a nontraditional student, so she could combine her two passions of teaching and writing in the university classroom, teaching creative, academic, and business writing.

She's a screenwriter, author, editor, and writing coach, who's been published across the genres, in multiple media, both traditionally and as an indie publisher.

Today, she lives in Michigan and writes full time. Her greatest joy after publishing books of fiction, nonfiction, and screenplays is helping other writers. When not writing, she enjoys movies, jigsaw puzzles, the seasons, and dining with friends and family.

Follow Dr. Diana

Follow links to Diana's social media and blogs from her website at sharpenedpencilsproductions.com. The social media icons are in the header.

There, you can sign up for her announcement-only newsletter, by clicking on the last menu tab located in the header.

Also by Diana Stout

Thriller

Harbor House: Deadly Intentions

Nonfiction

CPE: Character, Plot & Emotion
CPE Workbook
Finding Your Fire & Keeping It Hot
The Super Simple Easy Basic Cookbook

Screenplays published as books

David & Goliath
Charlie's Christmas Carole

Epic Fantasy

Grendel's Mother

Romance

Determined Hearts
Love's New Beginnings
Tomorrow's Wish for Love
Shattered Dreams #1
Burning Desire #2
Arrested Pleasures #3
Buried Hearts #4
Tangled Passions #5
Reserved Yearnings #6
Sweet Cravings #7
Laurel Ridge: Seven Ways to Love (#1-7 bundled)

Literary / Short Story

Maggie's Story

Romance Anthology / Collections

Lost and Found (story contribution & editor)
Unlock My Heart (story contribution)

Author's Note

In April 2023, *Harbor House: Say You Will* was published as a short Gothic romance novella in the now out-of-print *Hearts Unlocked* anthology.

That story inspired *Harbor House: Last Blood*, a psychological suspense set 100 years later with the same family, same house, and a 100-year-old unsolved mystery, but the book was missing the earlier history, so I considered merging the two stories together.

As a split-in-time book, the original story's history is an integral part of the modern-day story, plus it provided two mysteries instead of just one. Thus, the story was retitled and *Harbor House: Deadly Intentions* was born.

May this story be a page-turner for you, where you gasp and go *Wow, I didn't see that coming.* Where you want to share your excitement with your reader friends, and want to reread it all over again.

Best,

Diana, August 2025

www.ingramcontent.com/pod-product-compliance
Lightning Source LLC
LaVergne TN
LVHW090551110826
845146LV00001B/104